STORIES I STOLE FROM LORD BYRON'S BASTARD

STORIES INSPIRED BY VENETIAN HISTORY

SARA WESLEY MCBRIDE

PUCK
PUBLISHING

For Manu, who embraces far too many qualities of his ancestor, including unknown children. Thank you for being Lord Byron's bastard and for inspiring these many stories.

For Lord Byron, if I could sip wine from the balcony of Palazzo Mocenigo with anyone from history, it would be you.

CONTENTS

INTRODUCTION

George Gordon Byron, 6th Baron Byron, simply known as Lord Byron, wrote to his London publisher, John Murray, in 1817:

"There is still in the Doge's Palace the black veil painted over Faliero's picture, and the staircase whereon he was first crowned Doge and subsequently decapitated. This was the thing that most struck my imagination in Venice—more than the Rialto, which I visited for the sake of Shylock: and more, too, than Schiller's 'Armenian,' a novel which took a great hold of me when a boy. It is also called the 'Ghost Seer,' and I never walked down St. Mark's by moonlight without thinking of it. And 'at nine o'clock he died.' But I hate things all fiction, and therefore the Merchant and Othello have no great attractions for me, but Pierre has. There should always be some foundation of fact for the most airy fabric, and pure invention is but the talent of a liar."

~

I completely agree. In these stories you'll find that fact inspired fiction in my alter ego, Alexis Lynn, the heroine of *Will Write for Wine*.

And at the moment when I fix my story,
That sea-born city was in all her glory.

Lord Byron
Beppo, a Venetian Story, stanza X
Published February 28, 1818

"I can not conceive why people will always mix up my own character and opinions, with those of the imaginary beings which, as a poet, I have the right and liberty to draw."

Lord Byron
Spoken to Dr. Kennedy in Cephalonia, Greece, shortly before Lord Byron's death.
My Recollections of Lord Byron and Those of Eye-Witnesses of his Life by Contessa di Teresa Guiccioli
Published in 1869
English translation by Hubert E. H. Jerningham

THE DEVIL'S BRIDGE

*M*arch 1622
Venice, Italy

THE GONDOLIER STEERED us down dark canals on a moonless night and rowed under a stone archway. Engraved on the keystone, lit by a hanging lantern, was *Ponte del Diavolo*, the Devil's Bridge. That morning, I had awoken to Death. That evening, I did not desire another visit.

The damp air clung to my skirts and hair. My bodice reeked of brine and rot. The gondola stopped. It rocked and thumped against a wooden platform. There were shouts and the clang of an iron gate sliding away from the outside water entrance of the Venetian palazzo. A flickering, fiery light illuminated the lancet windows overhead, making them look more like the gates of Hell than the inviting home of an old friend.

My chaperone had died in transit, but I held her travel journal to my breast as if it might guard my virtue as she had done. I shared my late chaperone's travel itinerary with the gondolier and he brought me to this place, a gothic palace in the center of Venice. The facade loomed over me with frescoes of dead animals from a pleasure hunt. The water level displayed a painted garden of thorny vines with red poppies and white lilies, their petals and stems flaking off into the canal.

The gondolier spoke in an odd Italian dialect to the house servant. The cut of the servant's coat differed from that of my English house servants; the lines were curved and the bottom edges weighted with buttons. He nodded at me with a slight sneer. Had I imagined the sneer? It was dark, the gondola's lantern reflected off the water, distorting my perceptions.

The servant offered his hand as I stepped out of the boat, but I refused it, holding up my skirts instead. My two leather bags were deposited in the entryway of the palace. The servant withdrew several coins from a bag around his waist and paid the gondolier who smiled appreciatively, a little too appreciatively.

The servant ushered me inside and secured the sliding set of heavy bars across the canal entrance, as if I was entering a prison. He closed the large wooden doors, plunging us into darkness, except for a wall mounted burning torch that sat in an ornately carved iron ring. It resembled a shriveled hand of a corpse with long fingernails. Not that I, in my short twenty years of aristocratic British life, had ever seen the shriveled hand of a corpse, but I'd recently witnessed the dead body of my chaperone in the carriage seat across from me. Her skin was pallid, and her veins a deep blue upon her face and hands. Her hands looked as if they were reaching for something. A demon? An angel? The stench from her bodily evacuations certainly solidified the horrible vision into a haunting memory.

The servant picked up my two bags and jerked his head for me to follow him up the stairs, which immediately turned left and rose two flights to a brightly lit salon space. The fiery chandeliers overhead were the ones I'd seen from the canal.

The warmth of the room rejuvenated me and images of Death and Hell evaporated. Tall, graceful lancet windows, with their peaked tops and soft elongated arches, lined the outer wall of the room. But the room, this warm, enchanting room, with empty chairs, chaises, statues, art, books, game tables, and a blazing fire below a mantel adorned with silver treasures, was only to be walked through. As I looked around, admiring the opulence, I bumped into a table with decanters and glasses. The servant passed through the room without pausing and continued up another staircase at the opposite end. He said something to me I could not understand. When I inquired in Italian about my host, he ignored me and continued carrying my bags up the wide, elegant stairs, down a corridor past four fashionably sculpted doors, and up another staircase, this one narrow with a plain banister. Was I to sleep in the attic with the servants?

By the standards of 1622, I was an accomplished lady, well-versed in Italian, French, skilled at the pianoforte, and could pen a smart hand in my native tongue of English. I had lived most of my life in the court of King James and Queen Anne of Denmark. My parents had been ambassadors for the British empire, but two years ago, they perished in a shipwreck. My brother thought it wise that I marry a foreign nobleman to encourage a peaceful and profitable alliance between England and the Republic of Venice. A close friend of my family was the long-term Venetian ambassador to England, the nobleman Antonio Foscarini, who, now retired from diplomatic duties, delighted at the idea of introducing me to the noble families of Venice.

This palazzo I currently climbed through was supposed to be Foscarini's home, but I saw no portraits of him or his family.

The house suffered a silence that unnerved me. Even our footsteps were muffled when they should have echoed or thudded on the wooden floors. It was like a hole at the center of the house inhaled all the air and sounds of the living world and channeled it into the murky depths of the Venetian lagoon. In the corridor I currently walked, the six flaming torches did not waver. The air was flat and stale. On the top floor, the corridor only held one torch, and under it was a table with several stocked candlestick holders.

The servant set down my two bags. A spider scurried away as he lit a candle, handed it to me, and once again taking up my bags, silently led me to a room at the end of the dank, dark hall.

It was an austere, humid room with only a narrow bed, shallow writing desk, spindly wooden chair, and a single small window looking down upon the side canal. The room had no decorations or adornments.

There must have been some confusion. Was the servant aware of who I was?

All the furniture carvings were ordinary and square with no marquetry or embellishments. No paintings or even a simple cross hung on the white walls. One of the ceiling beams showed such obvious dampness and wood rot, I could observe it with my single, dim candle. The room smelled of mold and disuse. I doubted the room's window had been opened since the previous summer. There wasn't even a washbasin.

I lit the candle on the writing desk and turned to inquire if there had been a misunderstanding when the servant exited the room and locked it. A key decidedly turned and clicked. I twisted the door handle. It rattled but did not budge. I had been locked in. This was absurd.

After traveling through the night and awakening to the horrific odors and terrified, gaunt expression of my dead chaperone, I had spent fifteen hours escaping my misfortune via horseback, alongside my postilion rider, then journeying alone on boats and gondolas over a rough lagoon and through disorientating and pungent canals. I genuinely wished to wash up and enjoy a magnificent dinner among pleasant company. Being locked in a servant's room with no wash-basin, or—I looked under my pathetic convent bed—no chamber pot, put me in a more loathsome mood than I honestly thought possible. I wanted to stab my flaming candle into someone's eye.

However, there was nothing to do but to sit in my foul clothes, smelling my own foul odor, and embrace my foul mood. I couldn't even attempt to pick my teeth clean because my fingernails were so blackened from the day, I feared death if they touched my mouth.

While using my petticoat to carve out the dirt from under my fingernails, a petticoat I intended to burn, the door of my prison cell clicked. In walked a dignified elderly man with a sagging, pointed nose, a perfectly manicured beard, and an aura of viciousness that contradicted his apologetic words spoken in clean Italian.

"My humblest apologies Lady Morton—"

"Throckmorton. Lady Throckmorton," I nearly shouted at the man. "Where is Signore Foscarini? And why am I being held prisoner? Is it Venetian custom to kidnap a lady of the English court and leave her unattended? Before you waste your breath on false apologies," I grabbed my candlestick and stormed past the man, "I need a wash closet!"

I stomped down the length of the corridor and descended the stairs. The wash closet on the main floor of family bedrooms would be far superior to the servant's quarters. I opened the first door and found everything I required, including a full-length mirror. I immediately engaged the seated chamber pot. Afterward, free of my internal pressures, I now fully sensed the external pressure of the surrounding air. Sounds didn't travel, but stagnated. I couldn't breathe deeply, not because the air was thin, but because it was heavy. It wasn't just the damp of a foggy Venice night in March. An oppressive miasma hung in the air, but not of disease, of corruption.

I gave my hands and face a thorough cleansing in the washbasin. The gold threads of my right sleeve dangled carelessly. I untethered my sleeve and pulled it off. It hadn't been snagged or torn; it had been singed. Nearly the entire length of my sleeve had been burned. Surely I would remember such an occasion, but I could not. I looked in the mirror and saw that my entire right side, including a strand of hair, had been mildly scorched. I slipped my burnt sleeve on and retied it the best I could without the assistance of a lady's maid and exited the wash closet to assault my host.

The servant who had carried my bags stood in the corridor and gestured for me to follow him. He led me to the warm, comfortable salon. The vicious, bearded man stood near the window overlooking the canal. He did not turn to face me, but spoke in a clipped, efficient manner. "I am Antonio Priuli, Doge of Venice. When your host,

Foscarini, returned from England, Doge Bembo saw it fit to arrest Foscarini under suspicion of supplying the Spanish with state secrets. After three years of rotting in a prison cell, writing long, languid love letters to your queen, Doge Bembo was killed by the Spanish, then Doge Donato, after only a month in office, was also found dead. I then became doge, and in the desire to survive my reign more than 35 days, chose to release Foscarini. But you must now understand why I am suspicious of any foreign person entering Venice, alone, disguised as a proper lady of the court, but oddly lacking a chaperone or retinue, and displaying Foscarini's address as a place of residence."

He turned to face me and something flashed in his eyes. A moment of an unnatural black shine, or perhaps the fire opposite him reflected at me. Regardless, this man did not trust me, did not like me, and would happily throw my poisoned body into the fireplace.

"Perhaps you would like some refreshment? And then you may explain why I should not drown you in the lagoon before you murder me with that dagger hidden up your sleeve."

I reached for the shoulder tethers of my right sleeve and felt the handle of my slim dagger poking upward from under the white silk of my undershirt. I must have jostled it when I slipped my sleeve back on. What a fool I was to lose all sense of the armband holding a dagger to my upper arm. But upon entering this palazzo, my entire person felt strange and lost. Every part of me was weighed down and my senses dulled. I saw the doge walk across the room, but his image left streaks of color in the air as if he was simultaneously at the window and the drink table. I heard wine being poured before I saw it flow into the glass. Then in a moment, everything focused, and sights, sounds, and smells all synchronized.

"I desire no wine, thank you," I said.

"If you do not drink it, I should think it poisoned. A task easily achieved upon your entry when you followed my servant through the room."

My instinct wanted my feet to carry me as far away from this man as possible, but I forced myself to stand firm. "If you force it upon me, *I* should think it poisoned."

"How thrilling. Which one of us shall drink first?" Doge Priuli said. "What intriguing games they teach you in the court of King James." He threw the wine glass into the fireplace. It shattered against the brick and hissed in the flames. Then he threw the entire wine decanter into the fireplace. Then all the decanters, one after another, each one shattering and hissing. I tried not to flinch with each act of violence, but he became more ferocious with each object. Then he threw the table to its side with all the remaining glassware scattering to the floor and the table legs splintering.

I drew my dagger.

His face filled with rage, and horns protruded from his head. He marched directly toward me.

"But fear not." The normal, dignified bearded man stood by the window and gracefully walked toward the fully intact drink table. "I already had the wine disposed of and refilled while you were in your room." He poured a glass of wine and offered it to me.

I waved my dagger in the air, hunting for the demon that had stood in front of me. What had just happened? Had I already been poisoned?

"There is no need for swordplay," he continued. "I can tell you are untrained in the arts of self-defense. But here, look, it is only wine. I will drink first." He sipped from both glasses and again offered me the wine. "But Lady Throckmorton, I must insist that you please set down your dagger while drinking wine. I've lived in Venice far too long and have learned that the two together always result in a damaging red stain of some sort."

I frantically studied the room, the fireplace, the table, the windows. There were no red stains on the bricks of the fire, no splintered wood or shattered glass on the hearth, the floor planks were unscathed, the clothing of the doge was neither wrinkled, burnt, or stained, and the doge himself clearly had no horns protruding from his head.

Waking up to my dead chaperone had been a shock, followed by a stressful day of transport, and ending with a prison sentence. Perhaps the strain and anxiety of the day had caused me to hallucinate?

Perhaps I just needed food, wine, and a good night's sleep? I could start with the wine.

I dropped my dagger on a nearby chair. The doge's servant picked it up. I took the offered wine and thanked him. I sipped it. My breath failed to stall in my chest and my vision did not falter. I sipped more. And then I drank the entire glass. The doge's eyebrows shot upwards and he poured me another glass. He asked his servant to bring up a tray for a late supper. I thanked him.

"I have an offer for you," he said to me. I did not answer but glared at him over my wine glass. "Please, you may sit." I did not. If he was a demon, I needed to stay on my feet. "Or you may stand," he continued. "We will both remain standing if you like. Here is the offer: I promise not to poison you if you can bring me evidence of Foscarini's treasonous actions."

"What kind of evidence?"

"The usual. Letters, knowledge of his meetings, who comes and goes from the residence, maps of the Spanish fleet he probably keeps hidden in a locked desk drawer."

"You want me to spy on him?"

"Precisely."

"If I don't?" I asked.

"I think you've already seen how dangerous I can be in this world and the next one." He leaned forward, glared at me, and fire filled his eyes.

"The devil is in you!" I dropped my wine glass and ran from the room, descending the stairs to the boat landing from which I had entered. The single torch still blazed. I pulled open the wood doors and attempted to slide back the iron gate, but it wouldn't move. There was a lock at the bottom, securing the bars in place.

I reached my arm through the bars and screamed, "Help me!" There was a gondola passing under the bridge, *Ponte del Diavolo*, the Devil's Bridge. I screamed at the gondolier. He rowed directly in front of me. I reached for him and shook the bars, but he took no notice. It was as if I was hidden behind an impenetrable wall.

"Now do you understand?" The condescending voice of the devil rattled the walls around me. "Once anyone passes under my bridge, I control their senses, what they see, hear, taste, even the simple breeze they believe touches their face."

My mouth filled with blood. Literally. I bent over, retching out warm, thick, red mucus. I couldn't breathe. I coughed, gagged, clutched my throat, and fell to the ground. I touched the water. I scooped it up to my face, my mouth, trying to wash away the blood. The salty canal water lingered in my mouth and the blood stopped.

Something occurred to me. I splashed water into the entry room, surrounding myself with it. "You're fire," I said. The devil, cloaked in the garments and body of the doge, cocked his head at me. "When I ran by you, leaving my room, you burned my sleeve. You're a hell demon. You control fire. But you can't walk through water, can you? If I stay in the water, I'm safe. You can't touch me."

"Mortals. Always searching for logic when faced with the illogical. Would you care to test your hypothesis?"

I put both my arms and hands in the canal and started drenching myself with water and splashing it across the floor. It was icy cold and reeked of rotting fish or something fetid I didn't wish to imagine. My right sleeve burst into flame. I screamed as the fire singed my hair and my nostrils flared with the acrid smell. I dipped my flaming arm in the canal and untethered my right sleeve at the shoulder, tossing the sleeve through the bars, into the water.

My left sleeve burst into flame. I submerged it too, but the flame would not cease. My skin begin to sting and burn. My wet right hand pulled a second dagger from my boot, sliced my shoulder tethers, and I detached my burning sleeve. I sliced off the white silk of my under-shirt and tore it from my arm. My skin, even in the dim torchlight, appeared red and blistered.

"Oh, this is fun," the devil said. "I could force you to strip naked. However, I'm never cruel to my allies. Come, come. Considering your dress now stinks of sewage, it might serve our interests if you simply desisted in both your hypothesis and your attire."

As if magically summoned, his servant presented one of my leather bags and set it down at the base of the stairs. He opened my bag and peered inside, poking his long fingernails at my slips and corsets. Bile rose in my throat.

The devil gave a hand flourish toward my bag and said, "I will leave you to change into something less begrimed. You may sleep down here if you like, but I do believe the tide is rising tonight. Or you may join me in the salon for supper and wine while we discuss the details of your assignment. Do you like blue? I have a lovely blue room that I think you'll find most pleasant. And you may sleep with both your daggers if it comforts you. They cannot harm anyone of my household."

The next day, I was placed in the care of Signore Antonio Foscarini. Four weeks later, on a beautiful April morning in 1622, he was arrested leaving a senate meeting and accused of high treason by the Council of Ten. He was promptly executed on April 22, 1622.

For the Christmas holiday, Doge Priuli took up residence in Palazzo Ducale. He never returned to Palazzo Priuli and never again walked over the Devil's Bridge or passed under it. In late January, he issued an official government apology to the Foscarini family and officially ended the manhunt for Spanish spies that had cost the lives of countless innocent patricians. Living outside the cursed walls—or enchanted walls depending on one's perspective—of Palazzo Priuli, the doge's health declined rapidly, and he died only a few months later.

Foscarini's family never learned that it was I who had delivered false evidence to the devil. And why the devil wanted to murder an art collector remained a mystery to me. I think the devil simply took pleasure in playing games with mortals. Sadly, I found the devil's machinations to be quite similar to English court life. If a King wanted a man confirmed guilty, it was only a matter of time before a death sentence was passed. Also like the English court, there are certain bridges one should never pass under, cross over, or burn down. It was an accident my father stumbled into Foscarini's room instead of his own. It was another accident that my father recognized the Queen of England, Anne of Denmark, in Foscarini's bed. It was a bridge he never meant to cross.

I believe it was *not* an accident that my parent's next diplomatic assignment ended in a fiery shipwreck.

I have lived the rest of my days in Venice, married to a prominent merchant and nobleman. I look at my left arm now and there are no visible scars from that night. Yet, it only took me a night, a single night, to agree to bring about a man's execution. Until now, I've never acknowledged my own feelings that perhaps I held Foscarini responsible for the death of my parents. But the devil understood me, even if I didn't. And then I wonder if there was any devil at all, or perhaps only a scared young girl who read the fantastical name of a bridge and blamed an innocent man for her sudden abandonment to a foreign world.

INSPIRATION FOR THE DEVIL'S BRIDGE

*P*alazzo Priuli is now an elegant hotel (www.hotelpriuli.com) situated at the end of Devil's Bridge, *Ponte del Diavolo*, in the Castello area of Venice, near San Zaccaria.

Antonio Foscarini, executed on April 22, 1622, was a Venetian ambassador to London (1611-1615) and is rumored to have had an affair with King James' Queen, Anne of Denmark. He returned to Venice during a "Spy War" with Spain and was suspected of betraying Venetian secrets to Spanish officials. Upon his arrival in December 1615, he was arrested and held prisoner for three years under Doge Bembo, who uncovered the Bedmar plot which would have permitted Spanish mercenaries to march on Venice. In the midst of the crisis, Bembo died—or was possibly assassinated by the Spanish—and Doge Nicolo Donato reigned for a mere 35 days before he died. I believe he was assassinated by the Spanish, but have found no clear evidence for such a claim.

Antonio Priuli (1548-1623) was elected doge in 1618 and released Foscarini in order to monitor him and his activities. Priuli was a brutal doge who arrested hundreds of innocent Venetians suspected of plotting against Venice. Was he possessed by the devil? Probably not, but how Devil's Bridge earned its name is a mystery, so I took license and speculated that the devil enjoyed his residence at the bridge's end.

In 1620, Foscarini was elected to the senate. On April 8, 1622, upon leaving the senate, Foscarini was arrested and accused by the Council of Ten of meeting with ministers of foreign powers and of communicating the most intimate secrets of the Venetian Republic. The evidence was weak and Foscarini denied all charges, yet he was still condemned to a public execution for high treason. Why? The answer will never be known, so I had fun speculating that perhaps a guest of his, under her own volition or persuaded by a demonically possessed doge, provided false evidence to seal his fate.

By the end of 1622, Doge Priuli showed signs of illness. In January, 1623, the same Council of Ten revoked Foscarini's guilty verdict and reinstated the family's honor with a posthumous exoneration. His bust and tomb can be found in the Church of San Stae in Venice. There's more on Foscarini's final resting place in *The Masked Kiss*, another story in this collection.

Doge Antonio Priuli died on August 12, 1623, but oddly, I am unable to locate his tomb. I would have thought him to be buried in Santi Giovanni e Paolo (aka San Zanipolo), which houses tombs of 25 doges, but I haven't found him there. The art and sculpture in this basilica-sized ediface is amazing! This behemoth church manages to hide on the North side of the Castello and is off the beaten tourist path, but you should definitely seek it out. Alexis Lynn was delighted to discover another sexy *St. Jerome*, also by Alessandro Vittoria, but it was carved 15 years later than the Frari *St. Jerome* and looks a little tired: still sexy, but tired.

Two other Priuli doges, brothers Girolamo Priuli, 1486-1567, and Lorenzo Priuli, 1489-1559, are buried in San Salvador, the sensuous church where Manu introduces Alexis to two of Sansovino's sculptures and to Caterina Cornaro, the Queen of Cyprus. But apparently there was no space remaining for their Priuli descendent, or perhaps the family just didn't like Antonio.

Another source claims that the spy-hunting doge is buried alongside Marco Polo in the Church of San Lorenzo in the Castello district, but San Lorenzo has been closed for over a hundred years, only recently reopened, and I have not seen or read any evidence of the doge's tomb being contained within. They couldn't find Marco Polo either.

If you find the tomb of Venice's 94th Doge, Antonio Priuli, please write to me at sara@puckpublishing.com. Otherwise, I'll just have to assume he's buried in the depths of the canal under *Ponte del Diavolo*.

And like so many Venuses of Titian's
(The best's at Florence—see it, if ye will,)
They look when leaning over the balcony,
Or stepped from out a picture by Giorgione.

Lord Byron
Beppo, a Venetian Story, stanza XI
Published February 28, 1818

⁓

"At Florence I remained but a day…. What struck me most was … the mistress of Titian, a portrait; a Venus of Titian in the Medici Gallery …"

Lord Byron
Letter to his publisher, John Murray, April 27, 1817

STEALING GIORGIONE'S
MISTRESS

 ummer, 1508
Venice, Italy

TIZIANO VECELLIO GAZED at Violante di Modena draped in a white chemise with a heavy black velvet dress falling off her shoulder. The walls of the art studio had faded into a blur. The smell of paint thinner pierced his nose. He threw his pencil to the floor. He could not capture the texture of the material, the waves in her golden hair, her porcelain skin, her gentle brown eyes, and he absolutely failed to capture her vibrant, playful personality. His master had the gift of displaying his subject's inner thoughts, but Tiziano, so far, had only mastered motion and landscapes. To paint the thoughts of a sitting model was an entirely new challenge. And Tiziano yearned to learn Violante's inner thoughts.

"May I see it?" She asked him after she had dressed in her gown of yellow satin and smooth leather ties.

"It is only a sketch," he said, embarrassed by his lack of skill to fully encapsulate her beauty in his art.

"Violante, dearest," said the studio master, Giorgione. He put his large hands on the woman's shoulders and towered over her. "Do not pressure my students. Come away, come, come. Leave poor Tiziano alone to fret about his pencil strokes."

Giorgione and his mistress left the studio, but the twenty-year-old Tiziano remained for hours to fret about his pencil strokes. He transferred his drawing to canvas and attempted to improve it with brush strokes, but was not pleased with the result. He set the canvas aside. He promised to address it with his mentor tomorrow afternoon after they finished their day's work on the *Fondaco Dei Tedeschi* frescos near the Rialto bridge. The impressive five-story marketplace had recently been rebuilt after a fire, with the purpose of housing German merchants, both their persons and their wares. It was to function as a merchant house with a large dock under four palatial arches on the Grand Canal. Giorgione and his studio had been commissioned to fresco the immense facade over the Grand Canal.

The network of ropes and suspended platforms from which Tiziano and his colleagues hung was a daily attraction that inspired conversations across the city of Venice. Violante had posed for many of the muses and mythological figures exhibited in the fresco. She could wield a sword with ferocity, run while ladened down with multiple layers of heavy, colored cloth, look down upon others with angelic serenity, and most impressive, she appeared completely relaxed without any clothes on at all. Violante di Modena was indeed a woman with whom Tiziano could fall in love, or had already.

The next day, the fresco work required all of Tiziano's attention to manage supplies, color, wet plaster etchings, all for Giorgione to swing in and lay down the final touches. If the summer sun didn't dry the plaster fast enough, the colors wouldn't set, and Violante's angelic face would run and sour until she looked like a demon born from the hellish marsh pits that the city builders of Venice had proudly conquered.

"The clouds are coming in. The plaster must be thinner, or we will lose the entire day!" Tiziano shouted to his colleagues as he dangled from a rope holding a swinging plank.

"Keep the colors thick and bright," shouted Giorgione in contradiction. "There can be thicker plaster here, and here, if it means more vibrant colors. If the color is too thin, we'll need to rework the entire section."

Tiziano swung himself over to his master's platform. "It is already too wet. If the plaster is too thick, the colors could run and ruin the levels below. It is better to rework one section than three. The studio is already behind schedule."

"Do not fret my young friend. If we fall too far behind schedule, then I will entrust you to manage the *Merceria* facade on the *calle* entryway. It will not be nearly as magnificent, or seen by nearly as many as my masterpiece on the Grand Canal, but it will be all yours. Now, will that stop you from fretting?"

"I'm not ready," is all Tiziano could say between his mouth gaping open and closed like a distressed fish.

"Yes, you are. Now pass me that trowel, the pallet knife, and that bucket of red."

An hour later, Giorgione, a man ten years senior to Tiziano, asked that he be let down onto the dock. A narrow gondola pulled up and Violante sat inside. She waved to Tiziano and held up a lute. "I must steal your master for the evening. He is engaged by a nobleman to play and sing at a wedding."

"Will you come to the studio later?" Tiziano shouted down, knowing that although Giorgione was a respected artist, his mistress was not welcomed to attend functions of the noble class.

"Giorgione, what say you? Can I attend to your students this afternoon?" she asked.

"Yes," Giorgione said, as he untied himself from his seated swing. "I believe it might rain tonight, which means the day will be lost, and Tiziano needs to start planning the *Merceria* facade without me. You, my dear, must help him find a theme. Something with action and energy. For that is the only thing he believes he's good at. It is up to you to boost his confidence, for I have failed."

Tiziano heard this speech and smiled at the compliment. But he smiled more at the thought of viewing Violante in the studio that night.

~

"I'M GOING to drop this sword and damned be the person it falls upon," Violante said.

"No! One more moment. Keep still," Tiziano shouted while sketching quickly, making long strokes with his stick of lead. Two other students laughed from across the studio. They had already finished their evening sketches and were organizing supplies for the next day's work.

"The last candle is nearly out, and then I know not where this sword will land, but I'll aim it at you. May the goddess of darkness be your only protector, for I have forsaken you."

Tiziano laid his board, paper, and lead stick on the ground, jumped up and reached for the sword. "I take your burden to demonstrate my gentlemanly kindness."

"Or to protect your man parts," she said, as her arms finally fell to her side. She rolled her shoulders and stretched her neck. Tiziano set down the sword and began to knead her back and shoulders with his lead and charcoal-covered hands.

"Oh!" he said when he saw the charcoal he'd smudged on her. "I've made a mess of you. I'm terribly sorry."

"Don't stop. I've been in pain for an hour. Think of me as your living work of art. Sculpt my muscles."

The nub of a candle guttered and went out.

"Well," Tiziano said and laughed. "Now you can't see how dirty your shoulders and neck are." He felt his face flush at the many thoughts that engorged him while he rubbed Violante's shoulders in the dark. He wanted to let his hands wander to the front of her shoulders and down below her chemise—

"Here you go," a student brought over another lit candle.

Tiziano felt her lift her head slightly as she whispered, "Thank you," but then dropped her chin back down to her chest again while he continued to massage her shoulders. His colleagues were ready to leave, so he stopped and picked up his board, paper, and lead.

She continued to rub her own shoulders and neck, but reached down for a few stray papers Tiziano had tossed aside earlier. "These are very good," she said. "Who am I supposed to be?"

"Everyone paints Judith after she's cut off the head of Holofernes. But I want to show Judith's strength and not just her triumph. You are to be Judith decapitating Holofernes."

"After she seduces him and he passes out from drink."

"Yes!"

"And how does Judith feel about this?" Violante asked. "It requires a certain strength to seduce a man one despises, but a very different kind of strength to bring a sword down upon his neck, especially an unconscious neck. Could the same woman do both?"

"I believe you could," he said.

She didn't reply, but met his gaze. She gave him a sad smile, a curt nod, and walked away to dress in her everyday clothes.

"I'll escort you home," Tiziano said.

"No, thank you," she said. "Pietro Luzzi has already reserved the honor."

Tiziano looked at Luzzi, an inferior artist, as he adjusted his shoulder cape. Without a word, Tiziano snubbed the candle and exited the studio into the moist Venetian air.

10 MONTHS LATER.

The fresco on the Grand Canal facade of *Fondaco Dei Tedeschi* never had an official finish date, but after enough repairs and endless plaster flakes falling into the canal, in May 1509, Giorgione submitted his final bill to the German merchants. Finally, all, instead of half, of the ropes, platforms, and labor force were available to Tiziano and his team of artists working on the *calle* entrance side of the same building, the *Merceria* facade. The Grand Canal facade was nine months behind schedule. But the *Merceria* facade, despite the scarcity of equipment and labor, was only one month behind schedule, and Tiziano thought he might yet finish before the October deadline. He mumbled to himself as he frescoed the nude form of Violante near a third-story window. He lifted his hand to use as a model for Violante's. He smiled as he remembered a month before when she placed her hand on his. She had clasped his hand, leaned forward, kissed both his cheeks, and whispered, "I prefer that you see me as a serene, triumphant Judith. A woman with a kind and loving heart who would do anything to save her people."

One of the final repairs to the front facade was a large twelve-foot section over the main dock entrance. Tiziano executed it. Previously, Giorgione had frescoed a splendid angel who smiled down at a German soldier, blessing and offering protection to his trade routes. But much of the body of the angel had fallen into the canal. Tiziano frescoed over the section, and changed Violante's angelic smile into that of Judith, smiling down at the German soldier. The fact that Judith was stepping on the head of the giant Holofernes, and was larger, taller, and looking down upon the soldier, did not interfere with Tiziano's artistic passion. Tiziano had been completely focused on Violante's sereneness shining forth in the plaster, and getting the plaster to dry before the cool, moist evening clouds rolled in. However, Giorgione had to contend with a council of German merchants questioning the idea that a woman could intimidate a German soldier, even if she did wield a sword and slaughtered giants. Violante, on the other hand, glided by in her brother's gondola several times a day to pay her respects to the greatest fresco in Venice.

The top two stories of the *Merceria* facade were already complete. But those were short floors. Tiziano diligently worked on the details of the nude he vowed to finish today. He had chosen to start at the top of the building and fresco downward. If the plaster didn't dry and colors ran, it wouldn't damage any work on the lower levels.

Giorgione was a showman. He had wanted to display an artistic parade, to exhibit the fresco process to anyone floating by on the Grand Canal or standing on the Rialto bridge. While frescoing the Grand Canal facade, he had artists attacking multiple sections and figures, all simultaneously. Then Giorgione would gracefully, and sometimes acrobatically, paint in the details of the faces, the cloth, the hands. But he frescoed for the show of it, often applying too much plaster, too much color, and it couldn't dry before the wet, salty wind of the *sirocco* saturated it. If it didn't fall off the next week, it broke off three months later, when the salt crystals expanded in the plaster, causing cracks, allowing for a harsh wind to strip off the loose pieces of plaster.

Tiziano had made most of the Grand Canal facade repairs. He'd seen what his mentor had done wrong. On the *Merceria* facade, he worked steadily and methodically from the top to the bottom, from one side to the other side, like he was unrolling an enormous canvas onto the side of the building. His *trompe l'oeil* across the top fourth floor contained details that integrated into the entire design, accenting all the window edges. The third floor continued his mythological theme and introduced a few figures looking down upon the passersby below. The second floor, a taller floor, allowed him to really demonstrate his talent. He was eager to hear his mentor's thoughts on his work, but Giorgione hadn't been in the studio the past few days.

A month passed without meeting his mentor. He finished the third floor of the facade and before he started the bottom half of the building, he wanted to discuss his designs with his studio master. He visited Giorgione's home, but his servant said he was away. He asked the other painters if they'd seen Giorgione or Violante? None had. Although Pietro Luzzi, who Tiziano now pitied for his increasingly inferior painting skills, fresco skills, and drawing skills, oddly bragged that he had received no reply to his latest letters to Violante. "And before now, she always wrote me back. She appreciates my poetry."

Two more months passed and the end of August quickly approached. The mythological narrative of the facade was complete and Tiziano's team was now finishing the decorative details on the ground floor. He hoped to finish the entire facade by the first week of September, well before the requested deadline. But he hadn't seen Giorgione or Violante the entire summer. Tiziano met with the German merchants, created the design, executed the artwork, and

directed his team. Yet, Giorgione was accepting commissions, corre-
sponding and directing his other students, and asking them to meet
with patrons for portraits. Even Pietro Luzzi talked about a private
audience with Giorgione in his home. But Tiziano had received no
word from his master.

Tiziano followed one of Giorgione's servants and saw him
purchasing more food than could possibly be required for a house
with minimal staff. He cornered a servant at the back door and
demanded that he be brought to Giorgione.

"He will not see you," said the servant, his arms holding several
pounds of fresh fish.

Tiziano inhaled the salty, fishy smell. He took a step back, both
from the news and from the smell. "He has specifically said that he
will not see me? But why? This is ridiculous? It's been three months."

The servant attempted to close the door, but Tiziano inserted his
foot, leg, and upper body.

"No!" He pushed his way into the storage pantry. "Take me to
him!"

"I cannot!" said the servant.

Tiziano attempted to push past the servant, who threw his basket
full of fish on Tiziano's belted tunic. Fish juice ran down his wool
tights.

"I'm afraid I cannot bring any person to visit my master in such a
state of disarray," said the servant with a snobbish air.

"Tell Violante I'm here."

"Violante?"

"Don't lie to me. I am in communication with her brother and I
know she has been living here the past three months."

At that moment, Tiziano heard the most harmonious of sounds,
the graceful chords of instruction coming from the next room. It
was her.

"Violante! Violante!" He shouted and pushed toward the door
into the kitchen. There she stood. A beam of sunlight passing
through the window hit her yellow gown and burst into glorious
flame in his eyes. How he'd missed her smile, her voice, her smell;

she was salty. Of course, that might have been the fish juice on his tights.

"Tiziano." She stared at him as if he were dead and resurrected. "How are you here?" She pushed him into the storage pantry and nearly out the door. "You cannot be here. He is crazy with rage, with jealousy."

"Who? What are you talking about?"

"Giorgione. Months ago, he was walking the streets and people kept telling him how his work on the *Merceria* facade bested his Grand Canal facade. They did not know he could improve on something so wonderful. People were eager for him to finish the *Merceria* facade. First, it bewildered him, then, he, I don't know, he became distressed. As the weeks passed, the compliments grew greater. He became vengeful, full of rage. For an entire day he paced his room with a chisel in hand. He's locked himself away so he will not damage your facade. He has the utmost respect for the artwork. But you." Violante pushed Tiziano closer to the street door. Her eyes wild, she whispered, "I think he will damage you. He has said terrible things. I don't know what he truly feels or means, or doesn't mean anymore. But if he sees you, it will set him off. I believe he will kill you."

Tiziano had no idea how to process such a compliment mixed with such a threat. His master displayed such jealousy of his student's ability that he'd imprisoned himself to protect his student's artwork. Tiziano couldn't comprehend his mentor's emotions. It was too insane to process. And to see the terror in Violante's eyes, her face, to witness the tension in her shoulders and neck as she warned him that Giorgione might kill him, this terror she felt immediately transferred to him.

"Violante, you cannot stay here. He's dangerous."

"I'm afraid of what he'll do if I leave."

"You cannot be his prisoner."

"What alternative is there?" Her eyes welled up with tears.

"I've been offered a commission in Padua. Come with me."

"What?"

"Come with me. To Padua."

"He'll go mad."

"You need to get away from him."

She squeezed his hands and looked over her shoulder. She whispered, "When are you leaving?"

"In two weeks," he said. She bit her lip and looked over her shoulder again. "We can leave tonight if needed. We can leave right now." Impulse and fear took over. He grabbed her arm and pulled her out the door. He expected her to resist, but she didn't. Instead, she pulled away her hand so she could lift up her skirts and run faster. She looked over her shoulder, at her prison, and then to Tiziano. Tears stained her cheeks, but she ran and ran until they were lost. Tiziano called to a boat, and the gondolier paddled them to Campo San Polo, the campo near Tiziano's apartment.

"You must be quick. He'll send someone." Violante kept looking around like a scared child, afraid her jailer would discover her. "Does he know where you live?"

"No. I've only moved to these rooms a month ago."

Tiziano wasted no time and began filling a trunk with clothes, his few precious books, art supplies, and anything he might trade for cash. He inserted two daggers into his belt and a bag of coins. He threw two more bags of coins into the trunk and gave his final coin bag to Violante. "Hide this. It is for you in case we are separated. Hire an escort and return to your family home in the country."

Violante slipped the bag down her bodice, loosened her top, tied the coin bag strings within her corset laces, and tightened her top again. Tiziano paused his packing to watch. She looked up at him and relief washed over her face. "You still find me beautiful?"

Tiziano blinked. "Of course I do. But I've never seen a woman's undergarments before."

"You've seen me with no undergarments," she said with a raised eyebrow.

"Yes, but I've never seen you put them on or take them off."

She laughed. "Someday I'll have to teach you the finer details of women's undergarments. For artistic accuracy, of course."

"Of course." Tiziano blinked again and took a breath. He was running away to Padua with the woman he loved. With his master's mistress. Did he really know what he was getting himself into? He could never come back to Venice. He could never see his mural completed. He would never again work in the city that had raised him and taught him everything he knew. He had to start over. He had one commission. One chance to prove himself in Padua and to create a new chain of patrons. He could do it. He had his muse, the person he depended on most to create his art. He hadn't realized how much he had missed her. He contemplated returning to the studio to take the ten canvases of her that he'd started. But an image of an enraged Giorgione with a chisel flashed in his mind. It was too dangerous. Besides, he had the model. He had Violante. He'd paint new canvases.

He hired a boy on the top floor of his building to help him carry his chest to the campo and then to the water's edge. They hired a boat on a small canal in San Polo, and then they rowed away from the Grand Canal through the twists and turns of Venice's waterways toward the Guidecca. They would travel south across the lagoon to Chioggia and arrive by early morning. From there, they could travel by cart to Padua. It was a short ride. They'd make it in one day if the weather stayed warm. Then they'd be under the protection of Padua and the monks of Saint Anthony. Tiziano pondered how protective a holy brotherhood could be against an angry, towering Giorgione. What if the other less talented and loyal students stood by Giorgione's side? Tiziano smiled at himself. He'd have the opportunity to harm Pietro Luzzi. That might actually be fun.

Tiziano paid the rower generously and promised to trade rowing duties every hour. With luck, there might even be a breeze tonight, and the boat's small sail would carry Tiziano away from his home, from the city he loved, all that much faster. But for the moment, he sat on the seat of pillows next to Violante and cradled her in his arms. She nuzzled his chest. Her long blond hair mingled with his dark beard. He stroked her head, her hair, and kissed her forehead. They watched the sun set over the cathedrals, campaniles, palaces, and basilicas, and quietly, each separately, they said their goodbyes.

"Why do you smell like fish?" she asked.

⁓

September 1509, Padua, Italy

Tiziano Vecellio and Violante di Modena stood side-by-side under a great dome in the Byzantine Basilica di San Antonio, in the center of Padua. Violante reached her hand out and traced the cold figures of a bronze relief on the high altar.

"The perspective is amazing," she said. "But he doesn't understand anatomy. At least not female anatomy."

Tiziano laughed, heard the bright echo in the basilica, and covered his mouth with his hand. "Well," he whispered, "Donatello doesn't appreciate women as I do. If he'd had you as a model, he might have discovered the beauty of curves; the curve of the hips, the curve of the neck, the curve of the leg, the curve of the breast." He lightly stroked the curve of her side, from her thigh to her shoulder, with his index finger.

"Don't," she said and took a step away. "Not here."

"You're safe from him."

"Giorgione was never a threat, not to me," she said without looking at him.

"But you ran? You escaped him. I rescued you."

"I rescued myself."

"Violante, why this coldness? I left everything for you."

"You were coming here anyway," she said and moved to another bronze relief depicting Saint Anthony's miracle of the kneeling ass.

"But I left Venice without permission and I defied my mentor. I can never return. I thought …"

"You thought what?" she said from the other side of the altar. He couldn't see her face. He didn't know what she was thinking. They had arrived in Padua three days ago after a harried boat passage across the Venetian lagoon and a full day's ride in a horse-drawn cart. Tiziano had paid for rooms for the week and the two of them had collapsed into exhaustion. When he awoke, he was shocked to discover that she had undressed him and laundered his clothes. Even more to his surprise, was when she fell into bed with him and they made love. He'd been dreaming about making love to Violante for years, but as his mentor's mistress, she was untouchable. Now she was accessible and pursuing him. This was a miracle he chose not to question.

She finished circling the altar and again came face to face with him. "What miracles are you going to paint for the *Scuola del Santo?*"

He didn't answer. The brotherhood of St. Anthony had commissioned Tiziano to paint three frescoes in their meeting hall, the *Scuola del Santo*, based upon the merit of his Venetian frescoes. The same frescoes that infuriated his mentor.

"The brotherhood will not permit you to stay under their roof, but have offered me a nearby apartment. I will view it this afternoon. Will you come with me?"

"I like the rooms you rented."

"I cannot afford those indefinitely."

"Indefinitely?" she said, raising her eyebrows. "How long do you plan to stay here?" She looked up into the many domes above. Sun glinted off the gold mosaics. "It reminds me of Saint Mark's Basilica. You should paint your pictures and we should return to Venice."

"We can't."

"I can. My brother is there."

"I can't," Tiziano said, looking down at the marble floor. "Would you leave me?"

She did not answer and instead walked toward the north transept, where the remains of St. Anthony were buried. He followed her. She prayed quietly at the saint's bones.

"You pray for his soul? Giorgione's?"

"St. Anthony is the saint of lost things. Giorgione's soul will be lost without me. I worry for him."

"Then by all means, go back to him and leave me to my exile," Tiziano said and walked up the central nave, each footstep echoing louder than the one before, and the smell of incense stirring and wafting as he passed. As he stepped outside into the brightness of the day, he turned back to look at Violante, but the basilica's interior vanished into blackness.

The next day he settled into his new apartment and left a note in his old rooms for Violante containing directions if she wished to join him. He did not see her for four days.

He was roused from his drawing table by a knock at the door. The monks had been extremely generous to him, and he expected a barrel of wine to be delivered. To his surprise, he opened the door and there stood Violante with a trunk.

"Are you returning to Venice?" He asked her, eyeing the trunk.

"No. I used the coins you gave me to purchase new clothes, this trunk, and my independence."

"Your independence? You were no slave." He gestured for her to enter and reached for her trunk.

She waved away his hand. "Will you pay me to model for you?"

"Pay you? I've already given you a fourth of my savings."

"I thank you for your generous gift. Now, tell me, will you pay me for the artistic services I am able to provide, or shall I use my remaining funds to seek employment in another city?"

Tiziano stood frozen, both stunned and exhilarated by this new woman created by strange circumstances. He smiled at her and barked a laugh. "And where exactly would you go? You do realize there's a war throughout Northern Italy. League of Cambria sound familiar? I believe they've just taken Soave. The Venetian Republic may not even exist next year."

She scoffed, turned her back to him, and picked up the end of her trunk.

"Wait, wait. I am in need of a model. What are your rates?"

They negotiated a fair wage, and she walked in. "You may bring in my trunk." He reached his arms out to her, but she whisked by him. "Where is your studio?"

He flushed and rubbed the back of his neck. "The apartment is small. If I use the second bedroom as a studio, we will need to share the other bedroom."

She scoffed again. "I have my own rooms. I will no longer be a prisoner to any man."

He frowned at her and then hauled the trunk inside. He dropped it with a thud on the floor. "Open it," she said. He opened the trunk and in it were bolts of brightly colored cloth, daggers, swords, belts, a bible, a short staff, and various other objects. He picked up a series of chains attached to two metal bowls. "The scales of justice?"

"I am a professional businesswoman and must come prepared with props."

"You do realize how ridiculous all of this is? And who would rent a single woman a set of rooms?"

"Another single woman. As you said, there's a war on."

He laughed and smiled at her.

"And," she continued, "I expect a meal to be provided if I'm working more than five hours.".

"Of course. After all, the art from any master is only as good as the models he has to work from."

"You call yourself a master now?" she said with a smirk.

"I am now my own studio," he gestured around his small apartment, "with my own commissions, with my own model, whom I pay and provide meals for. Does that not define a master?"

She agreed and pronounced that they should get to work because she was already charging him by the hour.

It was several weeks before they fell into bed again. It's difficult for a man to spend all his time with monks and a beautiful naked woman, and for a woman to spend all her time with widows and a younger, talented man, without falling into bed together. He respected her advice, both artistically and in his dealings with the monks. He showed the brotherhood drawing after drawing of proposed frescoes, and they still had not settled on the three to be painted. They wanted Donatello's reliefs executed in fresco, but Tiziano wanted to make a name for himself. If he was never to return to Venice, first due to his departure without the proper paperwork and permissions, and second, the fact that Giorgione, despite being known as a lute-playing gentle giant, would throttle him with his enormous lute-playing hands, then he must make a name for himself here in Padua.

Finally, after two months, Tiziano had gained permission to paint his versions of the miracles of the newborn child, the repentant son, and the avaricious man's heart. Tiziano had rejected the monk's request for the kneeling ass or the congregation of fish. Violante told him to claim that he had no proper model willing to pose as an ass or a fish. This caused the monks to rub their chins, put their fingers in the air, look heavenward, frown, smile, but in the end, nod with laughter and agreement. There was another story of St. Anthony eating a poisoned meal and remaining unharmed, but Violante felt that her role in the painting could not be the focal point, thus, as any self-respecting model would do, discouraged it.

When Tiziano began to sketch his final drafts for the fresco, he noticed that Violante's body no longer matched his earlier sketches.

"I've merely grown fat," she said.

When they next made love, her breast could no longer fit neatly within his hand. He didn't mind the sensation, but he had not known a woman to gain so much fat specifically in her breast and her belly.

Weekly, he purchased cheese from the town's midwife. The war created so many widows, there was now a reduced need for midwives. He inquired with the midwife about Violante's weight gain and she smiled at him and winked. Her reaction completely surprised him.

"You will soon have a child," the older woman finally confessed after seeing Tiziano's distress and confusion.

"But it's only been two months?"

The midwife raised her eyebrows and turned away to wrap his cheese in a piece of cloth. She said nothing else.

Tiziano returned home with timelines of months and seasons running through his head. Five months ago, the *Merceria* fresco was half completed and Giorgione had locked himself away. Violante also soon vanished into Giorgione's household, rarely to be seen in public. He had heard of how women, particularly courtesans, had been able to prevent pregnancies, but Violante's world had been turned upside-down. Could she no longer gain the supplies she needed to prevent pregnancy? Had she become pregnant? Two months ago, she had run away with Tiziano to Padua. Did she know at that time that she was carrying Giorgione's child? Is that why she forced herself upon Tiziano a day after they arrived in Padua and then turned cold toward him? So that he might believe himself to be the father? Did she expect him to raise another man's child?

Tiziano looked up and realized he'd walked five extra streets past his apartment.

That afternoon, he asked her to pose nude for him. As he draped a beautiful orange satin cloth across her, he placed a hand on her slightly bulging belly. "It's Giorgione's, isn't it?"

She placed her own hand on top of his. "He's ours, Tiziano. He's ours."

He ripped his hand away. "How dare you lie to me. After everything I've sacrificed for you. I left Venice! I left my contacts, my patrons, my future. For what? For a small country town in the war-torn North? To bicker about the wonders of St. Anthony with a bunch of tonsure-crowned monks?"

"I did not know at the time. I swear it."

"You knew." He walked out of the studio and slammed the door.

He sat in his central room for a moment, rubbing his palms on his thighs, unsure what to do, what to say, how to feel. He poured himself a glass of wine and drank the entire glass. He poured himself another glass, but it tasted sour on his lips and he set it down on top of a sketch of Violante. At the angle he sat, it looked like her chest was torn open and filled with blood from the glass of red wine. He took the small cheese knife from a plate on the table and stabbed the drawing. He dripped wine onto the handle of the knife. It trickled down the blade, and soaked into the paper. Violante opened the studio door, draped in orange satin.

"I loved you," he said. "If you had been honest the day we ran away, I would have accepted you. But willful deception, I do not tolerate!" Tiziano walked out of the apartment.

TIZIANO SPENT the cold winter months alone in the upper hall of the *Scuola del Santo*. He mixed his plaster and paints and worked on the enormous walls before him. First, he frescoed himself and Giorgione eating poisoned food, but Giorgione didn't survive. He plastered over it. He painted a pond filled with fish, all eating bits and pieces of a human infant. He plastered over it. He knew nothing of proper fish anatomy. He painted an ass kneeling for the sacrament, then frescoed his own face on the head of the ass. He plastered over it. Two months later, he removed all the plaster from the wall and told the monks that the weather was too cold and moist to permit the fresco to dry properly and seal in the color.

He found the widow's home where Violante lived. She had not relocated. Tiziano knocked on the door and a woman dressed in dark colors showed him into a sitting room. Violante appeared, radiant and beautiful as ever. Her belly had swollen to the size of a small pumpkin, her cheeks flushed, and her wavy fair hair shined in the sunlight. She said nothing, but sat down across from him and placed her hands demurely in her lap.

"Every image I paint," he said, "I imagine your opinion of it. I constantly hear your voice pushing me to brighten the cloth here, increase the contrast there, reminding me of the light source and shadows. It is your face I trace in my mind to show me the shadows. I cannot escape you. I depend on you. You have been my guide for too long and I don't know how to paint without you."

She looked up at him, her eyes wet with tears. "I don't know how to be, how to be me, without you."

He knelt before her and took her hands in his. "Violante, I tried not to love you and failed. I will be yours, if you will be mine."

She nodded her head in affirmation and tears fell from her eyes. He thought she never looked more beautiful and attempted to memorize her face at that moment. He wanted to paint that face. This time, he wouldn't plaster over it.

"But I demand honesty," he said.

She nodded and smiled.

"Does Giorgione know? About the child?"

She shook her head in the negative. "My brother wrote me. Giorgione is destroyed. He paints me in everything. But he will not see me. He is too disappointed at my betrayal."

"By our betrayal," he said. "You shall not carry this guilt alone."

"I cannot tell him. It will only make it worse. He will never take me back, regardless. He is too passionate, too sensitive. Once betrayed, he never forgives. We are lost to him, you and me. I am so sorry Tiziano. It is all my fault. You have lost your mentor and your future, because of me, because of my fears, my concerns. I was too afraid of change, of losing my freedom. Being trapped in that house for three months showed me what being a wife would mean. It terrified me, even if I loved the man. No, you did nothing wrong."

"I dragged you from my mentor's home. I knew what I was doing. I'm not innocent in this. I was competitive with Giorgione, and Venice voted me the better artist. I thought that entitled me to win your hand. I would never have been so bold otherwise. I suffer from my own pride and ego."

"What you say is not true! You are all goodness to me."

"If you'd seen my latest frescoes you might think differently," he said with a rueful grin.

At the mention of frescoes, Violante's demeanor changed. "Your frescoes? How are they? Are you finished?"

"I have not yet started."

"It is nearly February."

"And the most terrible of seasons to work in fresco. I will wait until the child is born and then I will work. Until then, I want to take care of you."

MARCH PASSED and Violante moaned endlessly, and could not find a comfortable position at the table, in a chair, or in the bed. "It is settled," she said, "I must continuously walk, as all other positions are agonizing."

"It's raining," Tiziano pointed out the window.

"Take me to the basilica. I shall wander endlessly before the bones of St. Anthony and then perhaps I shall find that lovely brown leather belt I misplaced last week."

"Why do you require a belt?"

"To hold up this stupid belly of mine. My arms are tired?"

"You could once stand for three hours with a sword held aloft. And now you complain of your arms getting tired? My dear Violante, we shall have to create an exercise regiment after the child is born, to get you back into business as an artist's model. I plan to share in your income, you realize. I'm very modern."

She laughed. "Oh! Don't make me laugh. I'll water myself. Oh. Too late." A dribble of liquid pooled at her foot.

Tiziano went to the kitchen for a rag. When he returned, Violante was holding onto a chair. "I think you're going to need a bigger rag." At her feet was a much larger pool, and now it consisted of more than one color. "Get the midwife."

Tiziano ran to the door.

"Wait! Help me sit, first!"

Tiziano ran back to Violante, helped her into a chair, and then raced back to the door. He ran out into the rain, elated, excited, flustered, and dashed to the midwife's residence. The midwife gathered her bag and cloak, and followed Tiziano back to his house.

When Tiziano opened the door, Violante was breathing rapidly, her face flushed, her knuckles gripping the chair were stark white, and her eyes were closed. The midwife rushed in and began to organize her tools and the room. She pushed Tiziano into his studio and closed the door. But at Violante's first scream, he rushed to her, his eyes wide with fear. The midwife put him to work boiling water, grinding herbs, making tea, cleaning cloths, sheets, and rags. He felt like a painter's assistant, but knew the finished masterpiece would be so much more precious than any canvas.

Violante's labor continued through the night. The midwife began to tire and drank more herbal tea than Violante. At dawn, the midwife told Tiziano to fetch another woman. He returned with a younger, stronger woman who, upon entering the room insisted the windows be opened. Tiziano agreed, for he had not realized the stifling stench they had created in the small apartment over the last eighteen hours. When Tiziano finished opening all the windows, he saw grim faces on the two women. Then he was sent to close all but one window. He returned again and the older, tired midwife stood and waved Tiziano into his studio. "She may not survive. You must prepare yourself."

He was stunned. This thought had never crossed his mind. The idea of living without Violante, of painting without Violante, of eating without Violante, of waking up each morning without her fair hair in his face, and her smell in his nose, sent a chill through his body. He didn't know why, but he asked, "And the baby?"

"It is in God's hands," the old woman said.

Until now, he hadn't thought he cared for the child. It wasn't his. But he loved Violante and she was going to love the baby, so he would too. But to care for the baby without Violante was a horrible thought. He remembered his fresco of fish eating baby parts. It was a less horrible thought than Violante dying and the baby surviving. He did not want Giorgione's baby to kill his beautiful Violante.

Hours passed. Painful, terrible hours. Hour after hour of Violante growing more tired, paler, and colder. Her lips lost their color, her toes turned light blue, dark rings gathered under her eyes. Then there were cries, but not Violante's; cries of a small new life entering the world. Angry, tiny cries attached to tiny balled-up fists pounding the air it didn't want to breathe. It was a girl.

Violante, exhausted a moment earlier, found new energy and reached for her child. The midwives cleaned the baby, cut purple vines of flesh, stuffed rags into bleeding places, and smiled. Once Violante had her perfectly swaddled baby in her arms, her color began to return, her lips brightened with every kiss of that little round head, her toes wiggled and returned to a normal color. Tiziano arranged her hair into a halo on the pillow. He memorized the image.

Both Violante and her new baby girl lived.

A week later, Tiziano began to plan to return to the *Scuola del Santo* and again begin his fresco work. It was April 1510, but he had learned from Giorgione's studio to never promise finished frescoes by any date less than two years. It had only been six months. He would paint only a small section each day. Focus on the detail of faces or the landscapes. Take it slow and spend more hours at home with his new family than in the hall with his plaster and paints.

In June, a letter from Violante's brother arrived.

"He writes of Giorgione," Violante said. She was suddenly agitated, unable to sit. She paced the room as she read. Then she threw the letter in the fire.

Instinctively, Tiziano ran to the fire as if he could pull out the letter before it burned, but he knew with his first step that it would be pointless. And he didn't want to read the letter. He never again wanted to hear the name *Giorgione*.

Violante ran to the bedroom and began packing her small trunk.

"What are you doing?" he asked.

"I must go to him. I must bring him his daughter. He'll die otherwise. She is his reason to live."

Tiziano put a hand on hers and gently said, "No."

"He has a new mistress, and insists on visiting her."

"See. He no longer loves you. He's forgotten you."

"He sees her because she suffers the plague. Venice is stricken with it. He hopes to die."

Tiziano pulled his hand away. To imagine the large, gregarious man, his old mentor, wishing for death was a foreign notion. But he also felt jealousy. He'd won Violante. Now, from a plague-ridden city thirty miles away, Giorgione was threatening him, challenging him, testing his hold on Violante's heart.

"She is his child," she said. "If he sees her, holds her, he will welcome us back into his life."

"You're leaving me? After everything, you're returning to Giorgione?"

"What? No."

"He'll welcome you and his daughter, and I'll be left alone, in a country town, having given up everything for you."

"No, you should come too. I'll tell him everything you've done for me."

"Imagine that conversation. How do you think it will end?"

She threw the lid closed on her trunk and shouted at him, "What do you want me to do? He's going to die!" The baby started crying.

The next day, the city walls of Venice and Padua, and several other nearby cities, had closed to all outsiders. A week later, Violante was too weak to feed her daughter. Plague had hit Padua, and Tiziano worked while his neighbors died. The midwife found a wet nurse for the baby. Violante grew weaker and more determined to see Giorgione. Tiziano constantly found her sitting at the table, writing letters to Giorgione, begging Tiziano to post the letters. He read them, even when he didn't want to. She wrote of happy memories with Giorgione, in the studio, at salons, at parties, the moonlight view from his gondola as they floated down the Grand Canal and made love. She wrote that she would always love him and only him. Tiziano told Violante, now crazed with thirst and delirium, that he would post them. When she slept, he threw the letters in the fire.

After three torturous weeks, and her fever never breaking, her breath growing raspier each day, she made Tiziano promise that he would take their daughter to Giorgione. Tiziano promised, but this was like the letters. He waited for her to sleep, and when she never woke up, he let the promise burn through his heart and disappear.

He devoted himself to the frescoes, but the approved drawings no longer concerned him. He painted the first wall with the image of an enraged man holding his screaming wife by her long, wavy fair hair, and raising a dagger above her breast. The second fresco was a woman mourning the loss of her husband, while others looked down upon her. The third fresco celebrated the birth of a child, but the man the child is being presented to seems repulsed by the child. For months he continued to work and rework the frescoes, expressing his anger, betrayal, remorse, over and over again. He grieved through his paints. No matter how angry he was with Violante for threatening to return to Giorgione, he still mourned her loss. In November he received a letter from a fellow artist in Giorgione's studio. Giorgione had died.

Tiziano worked the frescoes again and again. But he finally began to come to terms with his grief. He started a correspondence with

Violante's brother, Alfonso di Modena. In the fresco of the *Jealous Husband*, he painted a small image in the background of St. Anthony forgiving the murderous husband and reviving the wife whom he'd stabbed. He painted himself as the jealous husband and Violante as the wife who was stabbed and revived.

In the *Repentant Son*, He transformed the mourning wife into a mourning mother with a repentant son, and St. Anthony healed the foot the son had tried to cut off because he had injured his mother with it. Tiziano still had nightmares of kicking Violante's once pregnant belly and killing Giorgione's child. But now they *were* nightmares instead of just dreams, or worse, desires. He even painted Giorgione into the crowd of onlookers.

The Miracle of the Newborn Child became a split background. The left side depicted the stones and archways of Venice and the right side depicted the countryside of Padua. The child crossed between borders. Again, he painted in Giorgione on the Venetian side, and himself and Violante on the Padua side.

In the summer of 1511, Violante's brother had written a petition to the council of Venice requesting that Tiziano Vecellio be allowed to return to Venice because of the great services he had performed in frescoing the *Fondaco Dei Tedeschi*. The petition was granted.

He presented the frescoes to the brotherhood of St. Anthony who were pleased enough. He received payment, collected Violante's daughter, and left Padua, never to return again. Alfonso di Modena and his wife had been unable to have children. They considered their niece a blessing and promised to call her their own.

After a month in Venice and drinking himself into a stupor each night, Tiziano finally fell into the canal and was so disgusted with himself the next morning, his clothes and hair smelling of sewage, he vowed to return to work. He returned to Giorgione's studio. The plague had killed half the population of Venice and real estate was no longer in high demand, hence, the empty studio sat, empty of people, empty of artists, but still full of canvases. He wandered into his corner, where he once sat, late into the night, burning through candles, working on paintings of Violante. He found the mound of melted wax on the floor. He saw ten canvases stacked under his work table, like books on a shelf. He pulled them out, one by one. They were all Violante. The brush strokes were a mix of Giorgione's and his own. How fitting. The two men who loved her combined together to immortalize her.

But did he want to immortalize the woman he loved who vowed to leave him, and then made him promise to save the man she had truly loved? Yes. Yes he did. She was a force. She was smart, bold, brash, loved art, and valued her independence once she had taken it. She deserved to be immortalized by the two men who loved her. And she deserved to be forgiven for valuing freedom above love. He pulled out the ten canvases and began to finish them. But one he could not finish; Giorgione had completely painted over it. Tiziano could see the ghosted image of his serene portrait of Violante as Judith, raising a sword and stepping on the head of Holofernes. It was the painting he had eventually frescoed on the *Fondaco Dei Tedeschi*, over the main delivery dock when Giorgione's angel had broken off and fallen into the canal. This is what had started Giorgione's jealousy. Tiziano should have honored his master's wishes and replaced Giorgione's angel blessing the German soldier, but his ego got the better of him. He wanted to prove to Venice that he was the superior artist. But where did that leave him now?

For three years he worked those other nine canvases and several others he found uncompleted by Giorgione. He enjoyed it. He remembered Violante as *Salome* and painted his own head on the platter. She was *Lucretia, Flora,* and *Vanity*. He painted her with a mirror because she did indeed love mirrors. She stood at the side of another model he barely remembered in *Holy Conversation*, painting Madonna and Child with Saints Catherine and Dominic and a donor. The donor was eager to finally receive the painting he had commissioned so many years prior.

In 1513, the secretary to the Venetian Council of Ten, approached Tiziano with a very desirable offer. The secretary inquired about a painting to celebrate his recent marriage in exchange for Tiziano to be given the position of *La Senseria*. It was an honorable position granting an office in the Fondaco Dei Tedeschi and annual salary. The position required Tiziano to paint portraits of the Doges and other occasional city commissions. It was lucrative. It was high status. It was exactly what Tiziano needed and wanted.

To please the secretary, Tiziano found an unfinished canvas by Giorgione, of Violante posed in a light blue gown with a red sleeve. She sat in an odd position. He thought it might be an early painting of Violante as the angel blessing the German merchants. The portrait reminded Tiziano why he had become an admirer of Giorgione's artistic passion and skill. Giorgione had captured Violante's inner thoughts. They were seductive inner thoughts that said, *If you do not behave, I just might stab you tonight and this red sleeve will hide the blood stain.* Next to Violante, Tiziano painted a sarcophagus featuring the secretary's coat of arms, even though he later realized that Violante's pose didn't sit well atop the ledge of the sarcophagus. He didn't care. He wanted to preserve Giorgione's image of her. Tiziano then painted Violante as he remembered her best, naked, playful, but with regret. He painted her inner thoughts as, *I have loved and lost.* In one canvas, she was both *Sacred and Profane Love* to both Giorgione and to Tiziano.

Tiziano even finished an early painting of his of Violante in a black dress, one where he felt the proportions were wrong and he had fretted over his pencil strokes. Now that he'd seen her pregnant, he felt that perhaps he might call it, *Pregnant Woman in a Black Dress.* But he didn't. To pay tribute to both their youth and folly, he titled it *Young Woman in a Black Dress.*

He found a remarkable painting by Giorgione of Violante stretched across a blanket and rumpled sheets, touching herself. She was a *Sleeping Venus,* but the backgrounds were unfinished. He painted Padua in the background. He felt it appropriate since Padua was her final resting place.

His final painting of her was in an elegant gown of bright blue silks and orange satins with her natural fair hair hanging loose and her strong glare penetrating the artist. This painting he decided to call *Violante.* He kept this painting for himself and hung it in his bedroom.

But once he was ready, once he felt himself fully recovered from his grief and anger, and had found his heart had completely forgiven her, he sold it. Each year, from 1511 to 1515, he sold three or four canvases. With the addition of the *La Senseria* position and its annual income, he saved enough money to open his own studio under his artistic name, Titian. He continued to decorate Venice for another sixty years and defined the world of Renaissance art alongside Michelangelo and Leonardo da Vinci.

INSPIRATION FOR STEALING
GIORGIONE'S MISTRESS

*M*y initial inspiration for this story came from Giorgio
Vasari's *The Lives of the Artists* (Oxford World's Clas-
sics Edition, 1991, translated by Julia Conaway Bondanella and Peter
Bondanella):

"Since many gentlemen did not realize that Giorgione
was no longer working on this facade nor that Titian
was doing it, after Titian unveiled part of it these men
congratulated Giorgione as friends would when they
ran into him, declaring that he had acquitted himself
better in the facade towards the Merceria than in the
one over the Grand Canal. Giorgione was so offended
by this that until Titian had completely finished the
work and it had become widely known that Titian had
painted that part of it, Giorgione seldom allowed
himself to be seen, and, from that time on, he never
wanted to be in Titian's company or to be his friend."

THERE ARE several historical references regarding the rivalry between Giorgione and Titian and a few that claim Titian ran off with Giorgione's mistress, and then both the mistress and Giorgione died of a broken heart. In truth, Giorgione died of the plague in September, 1510. He was long thought to have died and been buried on the Venetian plague island of Poveglia, but an archival document published in 2011 places his death on the quarantine/plague island of Lazzaretto Nuovo. More on the plague islands in the later story, *Lazzaretto Vecchio*.

There is a secondary source referencing a document dated 1511 from Violante di Modena's brother requesting permission from the council of Venice that Tiziano Vecellio (Titian) be allowed to return to Venice because of the great services he had performed in frescoing the Fondaco Dei Tedeschi. The petition was granted. I admit that I have not found this primary document, but do not doubt it once existed or remains buried in an archive. Such a document lends merit to the idea that Titian left Venice in a hurry, without applying for permission.

Among art historians, there has been five hundreds years of debates regarding attribution of many of Giorgione's paintings as to whether they are painted by Giorgione, or Titian, or both. Regardless of who painted which canvas, Violante di Modena seems to have modeled for many of them, thus bearing witness to a possible love affair with both great artists.

A fragment of Giorgione and Titian's central fresco for the Fondaco dei Tedeschi is preserved in the Galleria Giorgio Franchetti, housed in Ca' d'Oro in Venice. The fragment shows a female figure brandishing a sword. The face looks remarkably like Violante di Modena's when compared to the other paintings of her by Titian and Giorgione.

Titian's frescos in Padua are his earliest dated works, executed in 1511 as part of the decoration of the Scuola del Santo, and can still be viewed today. Likenesses of Violante, Giorgione, and Titian are all featured in the three frescoes.

The Miracle of the Jealous Husband
The Miracle of the Newborn Child
The Healing of the Wrathful Son

A PAINTING that also possibly features Violante di Modena is Giorgione's last painting, 1509-1510 - *Sleeping Venus*. It was finished by Titian. (Gemäldegalerie Alte Meister, Dresden)

Paintings first attributed to Giorgione, dated circa 1510, the year of Giorgione's death, were then reattributed to Titian and the dates altered to circa 1515. I speculated that all of these paintings feature Violante di Modena:

-*Young Woman in a Black Dress* (Kunsthistorisches Museum, Vienna)

-*Violante* (Kunsthistorisches Museum, Vienna)

-*Lucretia and her Husband Lucius Tarquinius Collatinus* (Kunsthistorisches Museum, Vienna)

-*Flora* (Uffizi Gallery, Florence)

-*Sacred and Profane Love* (Galleria Borghese, Rome)

-*Woman with a Mirror* (Musée du Louvre, Paris)

-*Vanity* (Alte Pinakothek, Munich)

-*Balbi Holy Conversation* (Fondazione Magnani-Rocca, Traversetolo)

-*Salome,* with Titian's self-portrait head on her plate. It is the same face as the man from the Padua frescoes of *Jealous Husband* and *Newborn Child*. (Doria Pamphilj Gallery, Rome)

LOOK UP THE PAINTINGS. Do you think the same model posed for all of them?

Of all the places where the Carnival
Was most facetious in the days of yore,
For dance, and song, and serenade, and ball,
And Masque, and Mime, and Mystery, and more
Than I have time to tell now, or at all,
Venice the bell from every city bore,—

Lord Byron
Beppo, a Venetian Story, stanza X
Published February 28, 1818

THE MASKED KISS

arnevale in February 1817
Venice, Italy

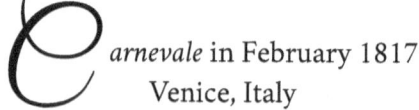

"FORGIVE ME FATHER, for I have *not* sinned," said Anthony Foscarini Olen, a British merchant's son visiting Venice on his Grand Tour to soak up culture with his friends. "My traveling companions drink, gamble, visit brothels, steal gondolas, which is no easy task in this city, but I do none of these things." The bust of his namesake, Antonio Foscarini, a Venetian statesman who, in 1622, was falsely accused of selling secrets to Spain, executed, and then exonerated a few months later, seemed a fitting representation of misplaced innocence. Anthony decided the bust to be the perfect creation to accept his confession. He pulled a six-foot pew over from the central nave to the small Foscarini family chapel in the San Stae Church. The scraping wood on the stone floor echoed in the tall, vacuous, empty space. Even the *Virtues* in Letterini's ceiling painting appeared to look down and grimace at the noise.

"Forgive me," Anthony said with a dismissive gesture to the

various portraits in the church. "Sadly, that is, and probably will be, my greatest sin these coming weeks."

It was *Carnevale,* and the English had descended upon the city of Venice for debauchery and delectables. "As you can see, dear Father Antonio, the church is empty, as everyone is off performing sins such that they might be forgiven tomorrow." As if on cue, two drunken men fell against the door at the church entrance, bursting into the central nave, followed by gales of laughter that reverberated through the columns and niches. Anthony looked up and Letterini's cherubs appeared to rejoice in the revelry. Then the men vanished, and for a moment, the sounds of the lapping water on the Grand Canal could be heard before the slow creak and resonate boom of the closed door restored silence.

"I think I am chasing an ideal that does not exist. Someday I will embrace reality. But Venice is the city of dreams and myths made tangible, is it not? Well, maybe not for you, Father Antonio. And yes, I realize you're not catholic. Or maybe you were? Maybe that is why you were falsely charged, falsely imprisoned, wrongly executed, and wasn't your body dragged through the streets, and then hung upside-down in St. Mark's square? If only I could be so lucky. You will be forever remembered."

Anthony held his hands together as if in prayer. "Please may someone believe I am worthy of such treatment?" Then he crossed himself in reverse, touching his shoulders in the wrong order, "*In Nomine Spiritus Sancti,*" then his stomach, "*et Filii,*" and ending at his forehead, "*et Patris, Amen.*" He glanced around the church with an expectant look, like a window might break, or the stone floor might crack open and a demon crawl out. "Nothing? I come to you in my hour of need and I get nothing. Dear father Antonio, I ask you to bless me with guilt I am undeserving of."

The silence of the church persisted. There was no whisper of wind, no flap of dove wings, no drip of water, no crunch of leather bottomed shoes on a dirty stone floor, there was nothing. Anthony pulled the pew a few more inches just to fill the silent void with the grating scrape of the wood. "Does anyone know I even exist?"

The church replied with more silence.

"You do not even look at me with both your eyes, but only in profile, as if you cannot see me, even in death, even as I stand here, praying to you, and only you, in an empty church during *Carnevale*. And yes, I'm aware that statement didn't fully make sense. I'm trying to raise a reaction out of you, Father Antonio, but you are a stone bust." He shook his head, stood, crossed himself in reverse one more time, and as he walked up the central nave toward the exit, he said, "You should have been a statue. But as a sign of my own insignificance, my namesake is only a small bust. Just a bust. Not even alone, but above another bust. And in profile!"

He pulled open the heavy wooden door at the entrance and turned to face the Foscarini chapel. He shouted, "Someday, some small boy will hit a ball with a cricket bat and break your nose. Then where will you be?" He waited for a reply, but once again, the church found comfort in supplying only silence. He whispered to himself, "Set in the garden and forgotten. That's where you'll be."

Anthony shivered as he remembered being forgotten by his family and servants when he was locked in their walled garden for an entire night, and no one came looking for him. He had been nine years old. Now he was nineteen. Ten years hadn't made him more noticeable.

He left the campo and walked down a dark alley, hoping something dastardly might happen to him. It didn't. He tried opening random doors, hoping to walk in on a crazy bacchanalia party lit only by a pentagram of candles and smelling of carnal succulents, but none of the doors gave way. He crossed over a bridge, paused at the center, and looked down into the canal water below. It was so dark, so inviting. The tip of a gondola poked out and then fully presented itself.

"You there! Come quick!" A lady in a black gown and veil called to him as she used the gondola pole to steer to the canal's edge.

Anthony rushed to the canal edge as the boat drew close. She reached up to him, offering her hand to assist him.

"You wish me to board?" he asked.

"Yes, quick!" she said. Her voice had the enticing lilt of an Italian accent.

At the moment his hand touched hers, his heart quickened, his mouth went dry, and all he could smell was her fragrance, rich with lavender and honey. He stepped down, the narrow boat rocked, and he felt her hand on his chest, pushing him backward. He thumped down on a pillow at the bottom of the boat. His hand spread over velvet and silk. The woman, in a black empire-waisted dress, pulled back her veil. Her heaving bosom came into full view, much like two pale half-moons in the dark night. A small silk mask studded with gemstones harbored holes perfectly fitted around the bright whites of her eyes. With a dainty, slippered foot, she playfully pushed him down onto the pillows.

"You stay there while I make our escape. Shhh. Say nothing." She used the gondola pole to push off from the wall and guide them down the canal. She turned the boat onto the Grand Canal where other floating vessels, hung with lanterns, carried all variety of people from lovers to musicians to pompous displays of powerful men.

"Quick, trade places." She threw herself down on the pillows next to him, breasts downward, so that he could not move without extracting his hand from her chest. "Your hand is cold," she said and giggled. "Now quick, row us to another canal across the way."

Anthony did as instructed by the beautiful, mysterious woman. He had never been commanded by a woman. He liked it. "Do you want me to go to the Cannaregio side, or stay in San Polo?"

An arm flung out and pointed across the Grand Canal to Cannaregio.

"Yes, Countess. I am your servant. Willing to do your bidding. Any bidding."

"Shhhh!"

Anthony took no offense. After all, the young maiden was hiding and it might look suspicious if he talked to a lump of pillows in a supposedly empty gondola. He found a deserted canal, bearing an ambiance of intrigue, and steered the gondola off of the Grand Canal.

"Countess, we are trespassing into the heart of the Cannaregio. The canal I've chosen is unusually wide. Do you know it? Stay down, there are mischief-makers about."

"Go left!" Came muffled words from amidst the pillows.

He turned left and immediately recognized the *fondamenta* they passed. He often purchased paints and canvas from a shop nearby. He passed a gondola moored to the wall. It snored. He looked again at the gondola. He whispered, "I believe Lord Byron has been rejected by his mistress once again." He heard the Countess giggle.

He turned down another canal. "Countess, you may sit up. It is quite safe now. The canal is abandoned."

She turned around, her veil pulled back and her beautiful pale skin, her smooth lips, and her pert nose all danced before him in wonderment. She had a mole on her left cheek, near the edge of her mouth, and bordering a dimple she displayed while smiling. She smiled at him. His heart raced. The gondola pole stabbed him in the side as it caught on the canal siding. He yelped. She laughed. Again, his eyes were drawn toward her dimple and mole.

"Why do you call me Countess?" she asked.

"What would you like me to call you?"

"Why not Venus, or Ariadne? Are we not in a labyrinth?"

"You are the sun that walks the night. With you in my presence, I could never be lost." Anthony felt every romantic bone in his body vibrating with desire and what he hoped was cleverness.

"I've been rescued by a poet. Do you write sonnets, or only spout them?" She adjusted herself on the pillows as if to get comfortable for a performance. A brown ringlet came loose and tickled the edge of her neck and bare shoulder.

Feeling bold, inspired by her playfulness, he pulled up the pole, knelt down beside her, and pushed the ringlet behind her ear.

"Truth be told, I am an artist. A painter. I know the classics and the myths, but am no poet." He reached up to play with the loose hair dangling from behind her ear. His thumb lightly stroked her neck. "Your skin is silk, like a delectable cream. You smile at me with beguilement. You are a mystery most exciting. You hold the power to lead any man into a labyrinth and he would gratefully accept his fate at the hands of the Minotaur if only he held the hope of embracing you in his arms, even if just for a moment. Do not tell me your name, as the mystery of you is so much dearer to me."

"Then let me be Ariadne and you, my Bacchus."

"Bacchus?" Anthony said as he was thrown backward by the boat bumping into the canal wall. She trilled another laugh, and he relished it, despite his awkwardness.

"Most definitely Bacchus!" she said. "Oh, this is my home. Will you assist me?"

He leaped up and once again took control of the boat. He steered away from where she was pointing. "What if I do not wish you to find your home in the labyrinth? What if I pray we may be lost forever?"

"Then what would we eat, and what would we drink?"

"Each other, of course!"

"Goodness," she said in mock fear. "You are Bacchus!"

"I only jest. Of course I will escort you home." With a sigh, he steered back toward the canal edge, near a bridge. She stood and straightened her dress. She reached for her veil, but he reached out and steadied her hand. She drew closer and again his senses were filled with her honey and lavender scent. She placed a hand on his cheek, the other on his waist, and kissed him. She kissed him. It was a long kiss that he melted into with his arms around her and her arms around him, as if they could make love while standing perfectly still and perfectly balanced in a narrow black boat. He felt the stiffness of her corset and was surprised. He gasped and drew a breath, then stared down at her breasts as they rose and fell. He touched his forehead to hers and quietly said, "Do you always wear such a contraption? It seems incredibly uncomfortable."

She gave him another small kiss and nibbled his lip. "Are you an innocent?"

"I have never undressed a woman, if that is what you are asking?" He looked into her eyes. They were dark and inviting. He fingered the top edge of her dress and the half-moons of her breasts. "Would you like to be my first?"

A balcony door opened above them and a candle revealed itself. "I must go!" She pulled away, placed a hand on his shoulder to steady herself, and he handed her up to the walkway.

"What about the boat?" he whispered.

"It isn't mine," she whispered back and pulled her veil down over her face.

"Will I see you again?"

"Paint me and I will find you."

And that was that. She vanished down a dark *calle* and into the interior of a complex of buildings. Anthony studied the buildings and all his surroundings. She must live here. He would visit her tomorrow, in daylight, when it was proper. Then he recognized the house in front of him. It was Tintoretto's home. The famous Venetian painter had lived in this house for twenty years in the late 1500s. Anthony laughed at himself and began to steer the gondola into the canal, happy to enter the labyrinth of waterways until he found his way back. One of Tintoretto's first commissions upon moving into the house was of *Venus, Ariadne, and Bacchus*, displayed in the *Palazzo Ducale* in St. Mark's square.

Was it all just a sweet dream of his unconscious trying to make mischief for him? Was it a wisp of *Carnevale* sinking its tendrils into his starved senses?

He smelled his hand, the shoulder of his waistcoat, and it smelled of honey and lavender. No, she had been real. He had encountered a goddess. He did not want to meet her in daylight when it was proper. He was not a man who did improper things in daylight, and he wanted to do improper things. He needed to become the artist, the poet, the Bacchus that his Ariadne and Venus desired.

He resolved to paint her. And paint her he did.

A year later, at the next *Carnevale*, Anthony Foscarini Olen now considered himself a local Venetian and strolled into the Church of San Stae to have a word with the bust of his namesake. A single six-foot pew sat waiting for him in the family chapel. But now in the chapel, there was a painting of great merit featuring a beautiful woman in a black dress and black veil, with dimples, dark eyes, and a mole near her smooth lips. She walked along a canal's edge as if in mourning, but her eyes were bright and searching. She reached under her veil to push back a loose ringlet of brown hair and her entire body appeared to be slightly uplifted, as if she had a spring in her step, a bounce of joy. Her black dress and veil signaled freedom, not sadness. A bridge and Tintoretto's home were in the background. On a balcony were flower boxes with honeysuckle and lavender. A small, black silk *Carnevale* mask, inlaid with several gemstones, lay at the edge of the planter box.

"Father Antonio, forgive me, for I still have not sinned. I hold too high a standard, and now I shall never find my Ariadne. But if one night, one moment can inspire such a muse within me, then I do not consider it a loss. I am a painter. And through my canvases I will be remembered. I exist. I have a purpose. Someday I will hold her again in my arms. I do believe that. But until then, I will keep painting. I have adorned you with my favorite of the twelve canvases thus far. What do you think? She is lively, no? There are many things I'd like to discuss about her with you, but not in a church, even if it is empty, and even if it is *Carnevale*."

The door in the central nave opened and a woman in a black dress and veil entered. Anthony stood and watched as the woman walked with a determined step down the central aisle. Each step echoed. Letterini's *Virtues* and cherubs sat taller on their faux plinths. The woman then turned left and walked straight toward the Foscarini family chapel. Anthony stepped aside from his small pew and offered it to her. But then he caught a glimpse of her dimples through the veil, of a mole near her mouth, and as she drew closer, she pulled back her veil. He looked into her unmasked eyes for the first time.

"Did you have to donate paintings to half the churches of Venice? This is my eighth church this evening."

Then she kissed him.

Then he kissed her.

And right there, in the church, under the bust of his namesake, Anthony learned about corsets.

INSPIRATION FOR THE
MASKED KISS

O n April 11, 1814, Napoleon's reign as King of Italy finally ended and a week later Venice was returned to Austrian rule. Over the next year, culminating with the fall of Napoleon at Waterloo in June 1815, the Austrian's successfully chased out the remaining French soldiers from the various lagoon islands and palazzos. Venice was once again available to host wealthy British partiers and became a required stop on the Grand Tour for young aristocrats.

Lord Byron arrived in 1816 and it was rumored that when his Venetian mistress was angry with him, she locked him out of the house. On such nights, he often slept in his gondola.

The silence and elegance of San Stae church is a favorite location of mine in Venice. I have often sat in the church and written a story while staring up at the bust of Antonio Foscarini, the passionate ambassador to England and Venetian senator who was wrongly executed for treason.

This story is completely fictitious, but inspired by the romantic impressions of a crescent moon over lantern lit gondolas passing beneath bridges between San Stae and Ca' Pesaro. What if one of those gondolas stopped and called to you?

"I have done some imprudent things, too, in my time; and in almost all cases opposition is a stimulus."

Lord Byron
In a letter to his friend, the Irish writer, Thomas Moore, regarding marriage.
My Recollections of Lord Byron and Those of Eye-Witnesses of his Life by Contessa di Teresa Guiccioli
Originally published in 1869
English translation by Hubert E. H. Jerningham

LAZZARETTO VECCHIO: A DOWRY FOR SAFFRON

*M*arch 1631
Ferrara, Italy

Costanza Alberti didn't know which was worse: marriage to a fat, worthless distant descendent of the House of Este in Ferrara, or working on a plague island in the Venetian lagoon? She chose the plague island. She secretly hoped that her betrothed might learn of her choice and thus feel properly insulted. But she knew him to be too dense to appreciate fully the dangers of a *Lazzaretto* during a severe plague outbreak and thus, would not be insulted and would simply accept the hand of any other poor woman cruelly attached to him by an ambitious father.

"Costanza Caducci," she said to a nun as she boarded one of five carriages bound for Venice. "I am trained in the arts of plague hygiene and it is my calling to assist those in need." Venice offered sizable donations to convents, and proper wages to any other able-bodied caretakers, to work at the plague islands, *Lazzarettos*, during the worse outbreak in Venice's history. By March 1631, the plague hospitals had been overrun and 30,000 souls, a fourth of Venice's population had already died. The only reason the hospitals still had any beds available was because people often died before they could be transported to the two plague islands. But most of the nuns and caretakers had also died.

Despite the long-standing tensions between Venice and Ferrara, the Duke of Este couldn't prevent nuns from pursuing their calling to help the sick. But anyone who left Ferrara and traveled to a plague-stricken city would not be readmitted within their home walls without a lengthy quarantine process. This would prevent Costanza's father from chasing her. Ferrara had closed its city walls six months ago. Her father oversaw the patrol teams for the East and South walls. Costanza, wearing a dark cloak and hood, exited the north gate with twenty-two nuns. No one questioned her except the nun who supervised the loading of the nuns and luggage into the five carriages.

The supervising nun placed a hand on Costanza's arm and said, "You are aware that you might never return?"

"I've said my farewells," Costanza said. She looked over her shoulder, saw the fires lit in the tall towers of the Este castle, and wondered when her father would discover her missing? She ducked her head and took a seat next to another nun who gave her a questioning look.

"It is my wedding day," Costanza whispered.

The seated nun nodded and reached for the silver cross hanging on her chest. "I remember when I married our Lord and savior." She paused, took a deep breath, and pursed her lips. She whispered, "It was not the happiest moment of my life, but I do not regret it." She looked past Costanza's eyes and under her hood. "You have not taken the veil?" Costanza shook her head and felt a ringlet of hair on her neck; a sign that her head had not been purged of vanity by the dull scissors afflicted upon all novitiates on their first day. "Even in the morning gloom, I can see your eyes are full of fear, your cheeks are flushed, and I imagine your heart feels as if it might burst from your chest. Yet the rose-scented oil you wear masks the salty smell of panic you surely have suffered the past few hours." The nun smiled at Costanza. Wrinkles grew at the corners of the nun's eyes. Costanza thought the nun must be close to her mother's age, had her mother still been alive. The nun nodded at Costanza and shushed her in a motherly, relaxing way. She whispered again, "Fear not. We will protect you."

For the first time since her mother had died two years ago, Costanza finally felt safe.

The muddy spring roads prevented easy transport and their coaches required three full days to travel forty-five miles from Ferrara to Chioggia. Costanza was welcomed at the three convents where rest and meals were taken. She felt a growing love for these women, especially the motherly one. When Costanza was fifteen, her mother had died. Her father and older brother took over as Costanza's primary companions and both were eager to use Costanza's beauty and intelligence as leverage for a good marriage that might promote their own ambitions within the Estes court. The man she'd been promised to couldn't discuss world politics, had no understanding of accounts or numbers, and from his misinterpretation of religious murals, she wondered if he could even read. If he was merely an idiot, she could take advantage of the situation, but he suffered perversions of the mind, spoke to her in vile whispers of how he wished to abuse her body, and never ended an evening sober.

Costanza told her father and brother of the vile things her future husband had said, but they ignored her, laughing it off. Her brother said that she should feel honored that her future husband felt comfortable enough to speak to her as if she was one of his brothel companions. Costanza did not feel honored to be compared to a brothel companion.

The night before her wedding, she refused to marry and held a dagger to her own throat. Her father smacked the dagger away and dragged her across the room by her hair. He pushed her torso out the window, still holding her by her hair, pushing her downward toward a stone courtyard forty feet below. He spoke from what sounded like a clenched jaw. "Your marriage is to benefit me, not you. Is that understood? If you cause me any more grief, I'll give that dagger to your husband as a wedding present." A few hours later, she had escaped into a carriage full of nuns bound for a plague island.

Three days later, Costanza now sat in Chioggia, in the company of women, and mostly unambitious women with little knowledge of politics or Ferrara senate discussions, and rather enjoyed it. These women discussed herbs, medicinal remedies, and how to acquire the ingredients for *Composito*, an oil used for treating plague. More importantly, *Composito* was used for the protection of those exposed to plague. Acquiring myrrh and *Crocus sativus* were of the utmost importance for their own survival.

"*Crocus sativus?*" Costanza asked the protective, motherly nun sitting next to her. "Is that saffron?" The nun smiled, her crowfeet crinkling at her eyes, and nodded to Costanza.

These nuns spoke to each other as if they were all business merchants debating Venetian trade routes. Costanza admired their ability to offer suggestions and listen to one another. From what she had heard of Ferrara's senators, no one listened to anyone else, and they each only wished to benefit themselves. But here sat a group of women trying to solve a problem that would benefit everyone. She marveled at them. But when she realized that she could provide a solution, she chose not to speak up.

A nun said, "Saffron shipments are highly valued throughout all of Europe. Venice is not the only city suffering plague. Almost half the population of Verona and Padua has perished, and every part of Europe is in distress."

"What has happened to the shipments promised from Naples?" An older nun asked.

"English pirates," a young nun answered.

The older nun nodded. "I'd forgotten, thank you."

"Is England suffering plague right now?" A nun asked another nun standing near a wall-mounted candelabra.

"No. Cases are few, and no buboes, so possibly not plague." The nun spoke Italian with an English accent. Costanza recognized her as one of the nuns from Ferrara, but this was the first time Costanza had heard her speak.

Later that evening, Costanza sought out the English nun and asked if she would walk with her in the gardens. As she had expected, she learned that the nun's mother was English and married into a wealthy Venetian family. Costanza confessed that her own mother's family were powerful merchants in Venice and could secure a shipment of saffron. However, it would mean Costanza would have to reveal her presence in Venice, which was precisely what she wished to avoid. She had escaped a father, a brother, and a betrothed fat toad in Ferrara, but she harbored no doubt that if her father learned of her whereabouts, he would drag her back and force her to marry.

"Then we must contaminate you. We must first secure your residency at the plague island, *Lazzaretto Vecchio*, so no one will not wish to remove you."

"But that means I'll be exposed to the plague before we've received the saffron shipment. Without the *Composito* oil, couldn't I die?"

"Absolutely," the English nun said. "Which is worse, marriage to a fat toad or death by plague?"

"Marriage to a fat toad, obviously, as then the death is miserable and slow, so slow. Plague is five days of fever, swelling, pain, and then you're dead. Sounds lovely. But might I offer another suggestion?"

"Please," the English nun gestured for them to sit on a bench.

"Perhaps you could write to your mother and father and they could apply to my mother's family, the Caducci?"

"The Caducci? I can do nothing. Venetian nobles protect their own," she explained to Costanza. "My family is not your family. Your family will see no reason to protect me and a group of nuns already committed to sacrificing their lives for the plague victims of Venice. But you are a granddaughter and probably a niece, correct? You are blood. And you have not taken the veil, thus you are still a viable commodity on the marriage market. If your father cannot use you for a favorable alliance, then perhaps your Venetian uncle will? Am I right?"

Costanza nodded. She knew her uncle would delight in marrying her off to another Venetian noble family in order to gain a seat in the Council of Ten or some such nonsense.

The English nun continued, "The Caducci, your family, they will fight to protect you. But they will do nothing to protect me."

"Are you saying that I must request the saffron for you and the other nuns, in exchange for me, my person, that I might be offered as a marriage prize?"

"That is exactly what I'm saying. If you step one foot on *Lazzaretto Vecchio*, you cannot be married. But if you *threaten* to travel with us to *Lazzaretto Vecchio* if saffron is *not* delivered to the island, then your uncle will insist saffron must be delivered to the island, and we will all live."

"And if I choose not to write to my family requesting saffron?"

"Then we will all die and it will be on your conscience. Whatever you believe, and regardless of how long, or short, a life you lead, every single nun in there that freely breathes air now, when their lungs fill with plague and they gasp their last breath, they will continue gasping in your dreams. Every one of them, including me, will haunt you. And if you think that we are young, we are strong, and no one from Ferrara dies of plague, then think of the nuns that traveled to Verona and Padua to assist those cities. Where are they now? Did they return to Ferrara? No, they died. But at least Verona and Padua have land where their bodies can be properly buried on consecrated soil. Where do you think the bodies are buried in Venice? In the vast fields of empty land? No, every bit of land reclaimed from the lagoon is precious. Our bodies will be washed out to sea, promised to never find rest, to never find peace. And who will our wandering soul blame? You. Because you could have saved us, but you chose, you *deliberately* chose to benefit yourself and condemn the rest of us. So we will haunt you."

Costanza stood up from the bench and looked at her companion in horror.

The English nun continued, "Now, I ask you again, which is worse? Marriage to a *Venetian* toad, or life on a plague island haunted by twenty-two dead nuns, or death of the plague and twenty-two vengeful souls all seeking to make your eternity more miserable than any hell the devil could ever create for you?"

Costanza turned and walked away. The air was moist on her face and the fog thick enough that she couldn't see the end of the garden path. But anywhere was safer than here. Here, she would be found and forced to marry. She needed to escape, to be lost. She needed to find a road, any road, and walk to the next town, secure a horse, and disappear. She heard footsteps running up behind her and quickened her pace.

"Where are you going?" The English nun shouted at her.

Costanza didn't answer. She hoped the fog would close in behind her and make the convent vanish from all around her. She ran into the garden wall. To her right was an arched wooden door. She opened the latch.

"I'll tell the other sisters," the English nun shouted.

Costanza stepped through the gate into a thick fog and blackness. The moon was still full, but thick clouds blocked its heavenly light. She stood on a muddy road facing a dense forest.

"Should you die tonight, we will still haunt you. If you leave this garden, then you have chosen to kill all of us. Is that who you are? Are you a murderess? I don't think so. You came to me because you wanted to help. If you sacrifice yourself to marriage, you can help all of us."

Costanza stood under the open arch of the gate, staring into the dark forest across the road. She desperately tried to see a path through the woods, a passage that might lead to safety. But there wasn't a path. Even in the fog and the darkness, she was certain the only road to travel was the one she stood upon and it would hide nothing. Costanza turned and said, "You are women committed to protecting the less fortunate and aiding the sick. I admire you." She stepped back into the walled garden and found the face of English nun. "I sought you out for my own protection under the full knowledge that I would probably die, but I would die doing something valuable and good. I would die alongside sisters who truly loved me." Costanza already knew what the English nun would say to this.

"But you can never be one of us, a sister. You can never take the veil if you are to remain valuable to your family; someone who your family will secure a shipment of saffron in order to protect. If you want to be valuable and do something good, then secure a shipment of saffron for not just us, the twenty-two nuns sacrificing the rest of their days to a plague island, but also for the families of Venice, the patients, the people who need the saffron for treatment. The Caducci will sacrifice the profit of one shipment in order to use you to gain a foothold into another noble family, and your sacrifice will be spoken of and valued by all on the island, both alive and dead. You will find protection in the wandering souls from *Lazzaretto Vecchio.*"

Costanza slowly stepped further into the garden. Her arms felt laden with chains as she reached for the door and closed it. The latch clicked in place, sealing her captive fate. The forest and her freedom were gone from view. She raised her face and met the eyes of the English nun. She saw the nun regaining her breath. She saw relief on the nun's face. Had the nun been afraid? Had the nun made such threats because she was afraid to die? Were all the nuns afraid of the mission they had chosen? Is that why they were so adamant about finding a way to secure saffron and myrrh before arriving at the plague island?

"Are you scared to die?" Costanza asked the English nun.

"Venice is providing a payment of ducats for each nun. The more nuns from a convent, the more financial support a convent receives."

Costanza had learned that the twenty-two nuns were from at least three different convents. "How many sisters are you traveling with from your convent?"

"None. I am the only one."

"The only one?"

"My convent only required a small donation to repair some windows. I was asked to go."

"You were asked to sacrifice your life for window repairs?"

"Not everyone's sacrifice can be as noble as yours," the English nun said with a condescending smirk.

"Hum," Costanza said. "Maybe your sisters just didn't like you?"

As the nuns gathered for compline, Costanza saw that the English nun was going to make an announcement, but Costanza jumped to her feet first, and said, "If it pleases you all, I believe my family can secure a shipment of saffron for *Lazzaretto Vecchio*. My late mother was a Caducci, and we have made our fortune in saffron."

Gasps, whispers, and prayers of joy spread across the chapel from both the Chioggia nuns and the twenty-two Ferrara nuns.

Costanza continued, "Tomorrow, I will travel by boat to Venice and meet with my uncle and grandfather. I will offer myself as a marriage token if they will promise saffron for the plague islands."

"But you're a nun? Can you be married?" asked a Chioggia nun.

"I have not yet taken the veil. I had planned to. But I now see that I have a different calling. That calling is to protect all of you, you who I see as my sisters."

Blessings and "Praise the Lord" echoed throughout the church.

"However," Costanza continued, "In exchange for my sacrifice, I ask something from all of you. I wish for an intelligent husband who will respect me. I know many of you have ties to wealthy Venetian families. If you wish to survive this horrible plague, then you will write to your kind brothers, your educated cousins, your unselfish nephews, and ask if any of them might seek the hand of a Caducci heir with a generous dowry."

The abbess of the Chioggia convent asked, "This is highly unusual, but these are unusual times." Then she raised an eyebrow and asked, "How generous is your dowry?"

"That depends on how generous the Republic of Venice has been to your convents. If you wish to acquire a shipment of saffron, then each convent will forfeit half the donation received from Venice. The combined sum will comprise my dowry, and thus the prize for a lucky brother, cousin, or nephew whom I might find worthy of my hand." Costanza couldn't believe her own ears. What was she saying? Was she mad? Did she plan to interview potential suitors? Would the Ferrara convents actually donate half of their income to save their nuns?

"What if our convents refuse to pay?" asked a Ferrara nun sitting in the front pew.

"Then don't go to the plague island. Remain here," Costanza said. She saw several jaws drop at the suggestion of challenging them all to defy their convents, the convents who had sent them off to die in exchange for building repairs. "Venice will not pay the convent until you arrive, correct? Your convent has the option of receiving no payment or half a payment. My uncle can confirm that half the payment will come directly to Chioggia. After all, he is the secretary to the Treasurer of Venice."

The abbess furrowed her brow at Costanza, or at least the lower part of the brow, as her habit hid the upper half of the old woman's forehead. "You want us to provide you with a dowry and a respectable husband in order to secure a saffron shipment? But what if your uncle chooses to marry you to whom he deems the best political union?"

"Then he must provide the dowry," Costanza said. "He's a merchant, not a nobleman. He values money over title. If he can gain a potentially profitable alliance at no cost to him, he will choose to do so, instead of investing his own funds in a potentially profitable alliance."

"But what if he deems his own investment more worthy if he can provide an alliance with a *guaranteed* profit?"

I smiled at the abbess. She understood finance. But I understood my uncle. "My uncle does not believe any profit can ever be guaranteed. It is both a fault and a blessing in him."

The supervising nun, the one who organized all the travel to Chioggia, spoke up, "If I'm not mistaken, Venice is paying our convents 200 ducats for each individual. There are twenty-two of us. Half of the paid income is twenty-two hundred ducats. Your dowry, if all of our respective convents are in agreement, would be twenty-two hundred ducats. That is indeed a worthy prize to any family. I have a younger cousin of a mild temperament I would like to recommend."

"Twenty-two hundred ducats!" a nun exclaimed.

"I have a nephew," another nun said.

"My brother is always writing to me of books he enjoys," said another. "Do you like books?"

The abbess looked down upon me, for she was quite tall, and said, "I have a grand nephew from a highly respectable family that I believe your uncle, and you, will look upon with favor."

Costanza left complines with a skip in her step. She wasn't quite sure how it happened, but she had taken control of her own life. Now she simply had to convince her uncle to provide a shipment of saffron. She boarded a daily transport ship the next morning and was rowed across the lagoon to a Venice city entrance gate which checked her for disease and confirmed that her documentation claimed her to be traveling from an area free of plague. With her, she carried nine letters of introduction to brothers, cousins, nephews, the abbess's grand nephew, and even a young widowed father with an infant and a toddler who owned an excellent palazzo near the Rialto Bridge. The nun had pushed the letter into Costanza's hand and pleaded, "You must consider my brother. He is recently widowed and was wholly dependent upon his wife's confident mind. He is a sweet, loving father, but I fear the children are too much for him to manage alone. They will take full advantage of him if they are not raised properly."

Costanza arrived in the city by noon and called upon four of the families that had been recommended. She was received by all of them, usually with the master of the household raising his eyebrows when he reached the part of the letter that read *2,200 ducats*. She sat and spoke with four of the available men, but all disappointed her in some way or another. The fourth family invited her to stay the night with them, but it only resulted in their son sneaking into her bedroom and reading poetry he'd written. Bad poetry. Although she admired the effort, he confessed that his parents had encouraged the act, and thus there was no effort on his part to actually admire.

The next day she met the final five families, including the abbess's grand nephew, who did indeed herald from a noble ancestry and managed the customs warehouses for the city of Venice. He had survived the plague, as had many of his workers, and would not wish it upon anyone. He understood the value of the plague island,

Lazzaretto Vecchio, and *Lazzaretto Nuovo,* the quarantine island set up to receive and air goods, and quarantine ship crews for forty days. He believed that without those controls, the city would have suffered many more plagues in the past, and the current plague would be far worse. Costanza liked this man. She asked if they might have dinner the next evening, and he agreed.

She also liked the widowed father, but more because his two young children were adorable. The man himself seemed flustered and lost within any conversation about literature, art, or politics. Although he had become quite familiar with children's stories, fables, and how to cook polenta. He even offered to teach Costanza how to cook polenta. Costanza thought he would be a man worth befriending and assisting, but not to marry.

After Costanza's second meeting with the abbess's grand nephew, the two strategized on how to approach her uncle. Costanza sent a messenger requesting permission to call on her uncle in the morning, and to her surprise, she was invited to meet her uncle at the Doge's Palace.

"Am I to understand," Costanza's uncle said and passed her a glass of wine while they stood in an enormous salon overlooking the Grand Canal. He continued, "That you intend to align yourself with the head of customs for the benefit of the family if I agree to execute two commands; first, to split the donations to the Ferrara convents, rerouting half to the abbess of Chioggia, and second, I secure a shipment of saffron for *Lazzaretto Vecchio?*"

Costanza nodded.

"And what does your father say to all this?"

"I am your sister's daughter. As far as my father is concerned, I am dead. If you would like to inform him of the death of Costanza Alberti, I would be delighted. I am now to be known forthwith as Costanza Caducci, if it pleases you, and I intend to make all *your* merchant importations top priority in the city's customs house."

"My sister taught you well," the uncle said. He smiled at Costanza, and drank from his wine glass. After several minutes of contemplation, he breathed deeply, faced her, and said, "Yes, I'll adopt you. Done!

But as for the saffron, that might be more difficult. All my future ship-ments have already been sold and paid for. However, in a year—"

A giant golden door swung open, and a gilded figure with an odd yellow hat walked through the salon. "Caducci," he called. The uncle raised his hand and caught the Doge's attention. The Doge approached him. Costanza noticed the strange looks and attention their little corner was now receiving. Why did the Doge not send a messenger to invite the uncle into his chambers for a conversation, which seemed to be the pattern of the day? "Caducci, I am very disap-pointed in you," the Doge said rather loudly.

Oh! Costanza realized the doge wished to publicly dress down her uncle. Then she realized what the Doge was going to say. The upcoming display of humiliation had been orchestrated by the abbess's grand nephew.

"You abuse my pirates to steal several shipments departing Naples, lay the blame on England, but do not share the stolen goods with Venice? I am very disappointed in you. Did you think I would remain ignorant?"

"No, your honor, your imminence, I mean, the goods have yet to arrive in Venice. I did not wish to promise delivery of goods if I could not secure them."

"Well, when will they be secured?" The Doge lifted his eyebrows and lowered his chin downward, keeping his eyes level with the uncle.

"Soon. Soon," the uncle stammered. "I am working with the master of customs as we speak. This is my daughter. The master of customs is her betrothed."

The Doge then looked at Costanza, gave a quick smile, and mumbled, "Congratulations." He looked back at her uncle and said, "I would like to see a bill of lading, a list of the winnings, before dinner tomorrow night." He flicked his robe to the side, turned on his heel, and strode out of the room. Several Venetian noblemen were staring at Costanza's uncle with looks of great disapprobation.

Costanza knew enough about how well voices carried in such an open space that she chose not to question her sudden status as Giacomo Caducci's daughter. She simply nodded to the various men who were now staring at her with interest. Her uncle gestured that they should leave, and she followed.

Once outside, she asked, "The shipments from Naples were not stolen by English pirates, but by Venetian pirates?"

He looked suspiciously at his newly adopted daughter. She continued, "One of the boats carried a large shipment of saffron, if I'm not mistaken. Could that be rerouted to *Lazzaretto Vecchio?*"

"I'm sure your betrothed has already submitted the bill of lading to the Doge's office. How convenient for you."

"However, if you would like to increase my dowry, I'm sure he would be able to reduce the weight of the saffron listed. I'm sure one hundred pounds could be skimmed off the top."

"A hundred pounds of saffron? That's worth sixty-five hundred ducats!"

"Precisely. After all, your pirates stole eight hundred pounds—"

"How knowledgable you are," the uncle said.

"So it's only right that you should see some of the profit. How many new merchant vessels can sixty-five hundred ducats purchase?"

"Twelve, at least," her uncle said. "Why?"

"That would be a lovely wedding present, don't you think?"

Costanza's uncle narrowed his eyes and looked at her. Then he turned away and laughed. He stopped walking and braced himself against an arcade pillar in San Marco's square. He continued to laugh. When he could finally control his breath and speak again, he said, "You are exactly the daughter I would wish to gain. I will write to your father declaring your death and disconnecting our families. You will marry the master of customs, and I will give you twelve merchant vessels to launch your family business." He hugged her. "Your mother would be proud."

Costanza personally saw to the deliveries of myrrh and saffron to *Lazzaretto Vecchio*, along with the other necessary ingredients for *Composito*. If the nuns followed the hygiene rules set down in Ferrara, of applying *Composito* to their skin, heating all clothing before and after use, spreading lime powder on the bodies and beds of the deceased, then they stood a very good chance of enduring the diseased environment.

Costanza visited the nuns in Chioggia and delivered the good news. Everyone was overjoyed to learn that Costanza was to wed the abbess's grand nephew, and that even though the nuns were all about to travel to their doom, at least they now had hope of surviving the plague and helping some of the patients instead of simply watching them all die. After dinner, she found the sister of the young widowed father and told her that she intended to assist him. She would find him a good nurse to help with the children, and Costanza promised to cover all the expenses of a cook, a servant, and the nurse. But she hoped to find a nurse that was young, attractive, with a sharp mind, and who might kindly receive the widowed father's attentions. The nun promised to pray for a happy second marriage for her lonely, scattered brother and gave Costanza a deep, thankful hug and blessing.

The English nun asked Costanza if they might walk and enjoy the night air in the garden. Costanza hesitated and then agreed.

The English nun said, "I am hopeful that the ghosts of *Lazzaretto Vecchio* will not haunt you. You have done well by us, Costanza Caducci. Would you like to hear another truth?"

"I don't know," Costanza said. "Do I?"

"When I met you, you were afraid and escaping something terrible. You didn't want your family to find you. And then I made it worse. I threatened to haunt you and to create an eternity more terrifying than the fires of Hell. I said that because I was scared. I'm still scared. My convent sent me away to die. My sisters ordered my execution. But you've inspired me, you see. You took control of your life, and I wonder if I might do the same. A week ago, you stood on the road outside this garden. You could have walked away. But you didn't. Why?"

Costanza gulped air. She walked to the garden gate and opened the latch. She stepped out and stared at the forest on the opposite side of the road. It was a clear night, with a half-moon and no fog. She heard frogs croak and bugs chirp. A gentle breeze caressed her face. The

English nun followed her out the gate and stood beside her. "I didn't run because I knew I would always be running. I would never be safe. I would never be truly free."

"Are you free now?"

"No. But I'm facing it now. And I feel independent, even though I know I'm not. I feel like I've taken control of my life instead of simply accepting my fate."

"The Bible says there is only fate," the English nun said.

"God doesn't believe in medicine either, but I do, and so do all those nuns about to face the plague." Costanza saw that her words did not ease the English nun. "Are you scared of death?" The English nun nodded. Costanza pointed down the road to the right. "Then walk away. Walk to the end of this road and in the morning, get on a boat. I will pay the half wage to your convent. Dismiss the veil, end your marriage to God—"

"Jesus—"

"Fine. And start a new life."

The English nun didn't look at Costanza, or say thank you, or hug her. She simply started walking. Costanza knew where that road ended and intended to detour her uncle's merchant vessel to pick up the nun in the morning.

As the English nun walked off, Costanza shouted, "Do you like children?"

The nun turned around, her face wet with tears that sparkled in the moonlight. She nodded and shouted a weak, "Yes." Then turned and continued walking, her black cloak eventually disappearing into the darkness of the night.

INSPIRATION FOR A DOWRY FOR SAFFRON

"*Sia laudato il signor Iddio non ci sono stati morti.*"
Bless the Lord, there have been no deaths [today].
December 24, 1630, in *Sant'Eufemia*, Venice.

⁓

THIS QUOTE IS from the opening of a *Nature* paper, "A digital reconstruction of the 1630-1631 large plague outbreak in Venice," by Gianrocco Lazzari, et al. Published Oct. 20, 2020.

⁓

I'VE ALWAYS BEEN FASCINATED by the European plagues, but when I read the above *Nature* paper, the effects of 1630-31 plague on Venice consumed my mornings for several weeks.

In the mid-14th century, bubonic plague killed one-third of the European population, up to 25 million people, and Venice, as a crossroads for international trade, lost half its residents. Imagine living in a bustling city of 100,000 people, and half of them die within 18 months. It would be horrifying and haunting.

In response to the devastating plague of 1348-49, Lazzaretto Vecchio was established in 1423 as the first quarantine island in the Mediterranean region, and was used to separate the healthy from the sick during Venetian plagues. Lazzaretto Nuovo was established shortly afterward as a place where ships suspected to carry sickness among their passengers or crew were anchored for 40 days. English acquired the word "quarantine" from the Italian term for 40 days, *quaranta giorni*.

Considering the 15th century world had no idea how disease was spread, the idea of quarantining the sick or foreigners arriving from plague stricken areas was very innovative.

This story takes place during Venice's plague of 1630-31, which killed a third of the city's population. Both plague islands were used to isolate and treat the sick, however, caregivers were needed to work at the island hospitals, mostly because, I assume, they also died of plague.

The Italian city of Ferrara had a long history of successfully avoiding plagues that ravaged other parts of Italy. They closed their city gates and screened all arrivals for any signs of disease. They insisted that *Fedi*, proofs, identification papers from a plague-free zone must be presented. Ferrara, starting as early as medieval times, engaged in public sanitation campaigns, sweeping away garbage and liberally spreading lime powder on any surface that had come into contact with an infected person. When an Italian physician, Girolamo Fracastoro, published a text in 1546 describing the "seeds of disease" as something that could stick to clothes and objects, Ferrara increased their sanitation practices during plagues and burned the clothes of an infected person. Removing garbage, spreading lime powder and burning infected clothing probably reduced the flea pestilence that actually carried *Yersinia pestis*, the bacterium that causes plague.

Many natural remedies were prescribed for protection against the plague, but a medicinal oil designed by a Spanish physician, Pedro Castagno, was written into Ferrara's, "*Reggimento contra la peste*," regimen against the plague. The oil, called *Composito*, was recommended to be applied to the body.

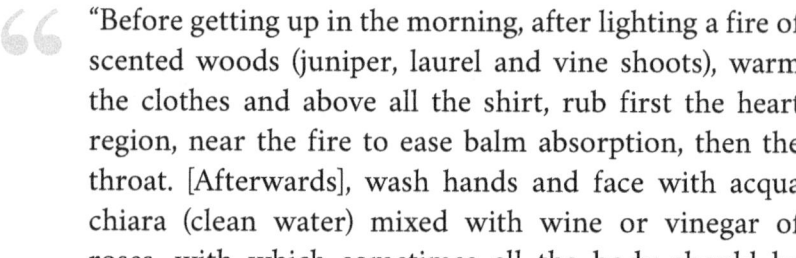

> "Before getting up in the morning, after lighting a fire of scented woods (juniper, laurel and vine shoots), warm the clothes and above all the shirt, rub first the heart region, near the fire to ease balm absorption, then the throat. [Afterwards], wash hands and face with acqua chiara (clean water) mixed with wine or vinegar of roses, with which sometimes all the body should be cleaned, using a sponge."

— FERRARA CITY'S REGIMEN AGAINST THE PLAGUE

The contents of *Composito* was never fully disclosed, but researchers examined the records of materials ordered by Castagno and determined that the oil contained venom from scorpions and vipers, and myrrh and *Crocus sativus*, which is a saffron flower from which the filaments produce the golden spice saffron. Both myrrh and saffron are known to have antibacterial properties, as does scorpion venom with the bonus that it's also a pain reliever. So basically, *Composito* was an early antibiotic and pain reliever combo. Pretty nifty!

According to census records, Venice's population was around 140,000 in 1624. By 1633, that number had fallen to 102,000. More than 43,000 deaths were recorded over just three years, with nearly half of them taking place between September and December 1630. The city of Venice began several public works projects, like the grand Baroque church, Santa Maria della Salute, greeting guests at the entrance to the Grand Canal. The church's construction began in November 1630 with the goal of keeping citizens employed and maintaining art and labor skills.

The city of Venice also purchased food for the quarantined, both in the city and on the plague islands. It is logical to speculate that in the early months of 1631, Venice might have asked Ferrara, a city with success at conquering the plague, if their convents could be paid in order to encourage *volunteers* to work at the plague islands. This story is fictitious, but the stage was set for events like this to happen. And yes, there were pirates at this time: mercenary pirates, government deployed pirates, well-dressed pirates, literary pirates, and a few pirates that claimed an island or two.

In my research of the plague islands, I was surprised by the lack of ghost ship stories haunting the Venetian lagoon. If you know of any, please write me at sara@puckpublishing.com. If you've ever visited the eerie lagoon island, Poveglia, the plague island, turned insane asylum, turned old-folks home, which now stands empty—less the chilling screams on foggy nights—I want to hear about it.

"Among them there is a portrait of Ariosto by Titian, surpassing all my anticipation of the power of painting or human expression; it is the poetry of portrait and the portrait of poetry. Here was also a portrait of a lady of the olden times, celebrated for her talents, whose name I forget, but whose features must always be remembered. I never saw greater beauty of sweetness, or wisdom; it is the kind of face to go mad about, because it can not detach itself from its frame."

Lord Byron
A letter written April 1817 to his publisher John Murray regarding a visit to the Manfrini Gallery in Venice.

A GENTLEMAN'S PORTRAIT BY A PREGNANT MAN

 ummer 1584
Venice, Italy

AS SHE ENTERED the art studio, passing under her father's engraved words, "The drawing of Michelangelo and the color of Titian," she brushed a hand over her cropped wig and checked that her doublet hid her feminine form. The smell of paint thinner forced her to bring a hand to her nose for several breaths until she grew accustomed to it.

"Marietta! Good, you look like a boy. Do you feel confident you can take the old man's likeness?" Jacopo Tintoretto put his arm around his eldest daughter's shoulders. "This will be no different from your past portraits. You are my most talented assistant, boy or girl."

"Can I put my name on the canvas?"

"Of course not. Do not ask such silly things. Boy or girl, you are an assistant."

"But I'm not an apprentice anymore."

"But you are of the studio Tintoretto. When you have your own studio, then you can sign the canvas."

"I'm a woman. I will never run my own studio. It is prohibited."

"There you have it," Tintoretto said, and shrugged. He picked up a bread roll from the breakfast table and offered it to her. She pushed it away and broke free from his arm. "Marietta. Wait. Why is it so important to you?"

"For the same reason it's important to you, Papa. To be remembered! To be recognized for your achievements."

"Very few female artists are remembered."

"But the one's who are remembered, they signed their name, their own name, not their father's name, not their master's name, but their name to the canvas." Marietta turned away from her father, walked to the breakfast table, and picked up another bread roll.

"See, you were hungry. I knew you were hungry," Tintoretto said to his daughter as he examined the roll in his own hand.

She sighed and shook her head.

Morning light streamed in from a low window and four young painters worked at a large canvas that leaned against a table. They were each painting background figures in Roman togas. Marietta waved to her fourteen-year-old sister who was working on the canvas. Marietta had already spent seven years of her youth painting background figures. In another corner of the studio sat a wooden podium with a chair. A woman draped in white cloth with her hair pinned up to mimic a Roman goddess, posed with a sleeping infant on her lap. Four more young artists stood at easels with pencil and paper. She waved to two of her brothers. Marietta had spent another six years of her youth painting portraits and religious iconography for the many churches of Venice. But today, at age twenty-four, her father was sending her out to draw and paint a portrait completely on her own. If she had been anyone else's daughter, such an opportunity would never have been afforded.

Marietta started gathering her supplies near the long canvas that her sister worked on. She looked up and noticed that her sister wasn't painting to the same scale as the other three apprentices. "Look here," she whispered to her sister. "Your figures are too large." Her sister gave a small yelp and stood back, eyeing the other sections of canvas.

"What do I do? Father will make me clean brushes and grind paint for a year."

Whispering, Marietta asked, "Do you feel confident you can set your figures in the foreground?" The girl furrowed her brow, studied the long canvas, and nodded in the affirmative. Marietta clapped her hands and asked the three other apprentices to come closer. "Look here. The Master asked that the canvas be slightly altered, but I can see he has forgotten to tell all of you, which is his way, of course. Do not blame yourselves. But look here. You can see that my sister has set her characters in the foreground, as instructed, thus they are larger. Please continue as you are, but be aware that any of her characters which overlap yours will take the frontal overlap, and your characters will be smaller and pushed into the background. Does that make sense?"

The three boys nodded and studied the painting. One asked, "Should I paint over the side of this man here, so the larger figure becomes the forefront? Will that help?"

"That is perfect," said Marietta. "Thank you for accommodating the Master. With so many commissions, he is forgetful. Well done. Keep it up and talk to each other. The canvas should look like one brush painted it, not four. I'll make sure you each get extra cheese this week." She winked at their smiles and raised eyebrows and then squeezed her sister's shoulder.

"Someday ..."

"Someday what?" Marietta asked her sister.

"Someday I hope to be as talented as the great Marietta Robusti. That's all."

"Someday I hope you will be, and that you won't have to dress as a man to do it."

Carrying a bucket of brushes, pencils, and paints in one hand, and a large canvas and drawing sheets under her opposite arm, she zig-zagged her way through the streets and canals of the Cannaregio until she found the Rialto bridge, the only way of crossing the Grand Canal on foot. The narrow wooden bridge was bustling with people. Each one carried buckets, baskets, boards, and one person with a bag full of very potent smelling tanned hides that reeked of urine. She tightened her grip on her own bucket and canvas and entered the fray. She followed a man carrying a wide basket of fish as she navigated the short, deep steps of the bridge, each step creaking underneath her feet. Her upper arm was tired of pinching the canvas and drawing paper to her side, and the doublet made the flat shapes bulk out awkwardly. Her arm wasn't quite long enough to comfortably reach across the entire canvas, and her fingertips ached from treading at the edges. The basket of dead fish wafted the smell of rotting seaweed and foul detritus into her nose. She heard the lapping of the waves beneath her and felt her canvas catch in the wind. She attempted to strengthen her grip but felt her fingers slipping with the tug of the breeze. She stumbled into a woman in a rough wool dress who carried a bucket of something white and gelatinous.

"Watch it there," the woman said and stepped into the center of the bridge and stopped. She set her bucket down and steadied Marietta. "Stay here. We are out of the way. Quick, switch arms."

Marietta thanked her with a nod and set down her supply bucket. Shouts could be heard in the distance, and grumbles resonated as the bustling continued with an occasional nudge. Together they maneuvered the canvas to Marietta's other arm. They both picked up their buckets to continue in their opposite directions, but the woman set her bucket down again. "Wait," she shouted. Marietta turned and saw the woman's hands reaching toward her head. "You'll never pass as a boy with your hair exposed." She reached into her bucket and took a finger full of the gelatinous goop and applied it to Marietta's loosening hair, then tucked everything back under the cropped wig. "Lard. That will hold it. But don't stand in the sun too long. You might attract birds."

"Thank you. Thank you truly." Marietta memorized the woman's face. It was a face she wanted to paint. The woman turned and continued into the Cannaregio. Marietta yelled, "Will you come to Tintoretto's studio? Please. Anytime. Tell them Robusti asked for you. Robusti!" The wind knocked against the canvas again. She stepped back into the lane of human traffic crossing to the San Polo side. She hoped the woman heard her. She had a wonderful face. It was both youthful and old. The eyes were bulbous, but plain. The features were complex, even without age lines. And she would never forget that finger full of lard reaching up to her head. Would her head really attract birds? She decided to travel via the interior *calles*, rather than the canal-side *fondamentas*; fewer birds. If she arrived without a wig, the job would be canceled, and her father would lose at least a dozen commissions for the scandal of sending a woman to paint portraits.

She checked the time on the 24-hour clock atop San Giacomo di Rialto, hoped it was wrong as usual, otherwise she was late, and smiled at the statue of Gobbo, the hunchback of the Rialto. She liked the story of Gobbo, and he was fun to draw. Tucked between buildings, the wind no longer pulled at her canvas. She felt relief when she saw her favorite crooked bridge at the Beccarie canal. Another bit of drawing fun. The crooked bridge set against the graceful lines of a well-built palazzo created a sense of opposites that she found cheerful and slightly comical, like Gobbo, or the 24-hour clock that refused to chime the correct time.

She arrived at her client's door, set down her bucket, checked her wig, shifted the canvas and drawing paper to the other arm, and used the iron ring in the lion's mouth to knock on the door. She loved that many of the door knockers in this area of Venice featured lions' heads. One day, she hoped to see a real lion. She did not believe she would understand the function of a lion's mane, the giant, useless ruff of fur around a lion's head, until she met one in person. Then maybe she would understand why humans attempted to imitate lions with their great ruff collars. Except humans obviously had the ruff in the wrong place. Why would anyone wear such a thing under their chin instead of behind their ears, like the majestic lion? For humans, it merely became an obstacle that trapped food and soup. She imagined a ruffled collar balanced behind a man's ears as if dramatically surrounding a monk's tonsure.

"Yes, sir?"

She couldn't see the speaker. Then door opened further and the servant leaned his head forward into the light, permitting his face to be bright and visible, but the rest of him was in darkness as if a lion's mane of dark hair encapsulated the servant. She laughed.

"Sir?"

"I'm from Tintoretto's studio. I'm here to paint the gentleman of the house."

The servant nodded and retracted his face as a turtle pulls his head into a dark shell. She heard his footsteps receding away from her and she grabbed her bucket and followed. She hoped she would not be required to paint in such a dark place as the entry hall. Portraits by candlelight were always more challenging as there were multiple light sources and the shadows continuously shifted. She suddenly decided that if there were no windows with good natural light, she would paint the old man in the kitchen.

The servant opened a door and gestured for Marietta to enter. There was a window! The room was paneled in dark wood, but there was a small writing table between two tall, slender windows containing beautiful, clear glass. Two of the walls were filled with books, and the third wall had a long bench with finely carved arms and an elaborate back. The bench looked as if it was carved from a single tree.

"Yes, you have observed correctly."

She jumped. A man dressed in a black velvet cloak stood at a bookcase to her right. "I'm sorry, sir?"

"The bench. It is one single tree. Nothing is a separate piece. Nothing attached."

"Miraculous! Might I ask who the artist is?"

"A sculptor of no great reputation. I believe he's much better known as a cloth merchant."

"Well, that piece is worthy of the Doge's palace."

The man opened his book and flipped to the front page. It was small, with a worn leather cover and easily fit into his hands. "I thought I might read while you worked. Is that alright?"

"Absolutely. Would you like the book included in the portrait?" Marietta asked.

"Oh no. I always think that's so pretentious. As if to say, 'Look at me. I can read.' I once saw a portrait of a dear friend and he held a book to his chest as if it was armor." The man demonstrated, folding the closed book into his hand and pressing it against his chest. "Like so. The funny thing is, I knew he could not read, as did most people. And even odder still was that he was not pretending to read, but merely holding a book. Was it a sign of respect for literature? A world he wished he enjoyed? A world he wanted to be associated with? Ever since then, whenever I see a book prominently displayed in a portrait, I always ask myself, 'I wonder if that man, or woman, can read?' Do you see how awkward that is? I do not want my descendants viewing my portrait and wondering if I can read. It is not what I want them thinking about."

Marietta liked this man dressed in a full-length black velvet cloak with a small, well-worn book in his hands. "What do you want your descendants to think about when they view your portrait?"

The man stood still, not a single muscle in his face moved. Finally, he stroked his dark pointed beard and said, "Do you ask that of all your subjects?"

Marietta sat down her bucket and her canvas and her drawing paper. She stood up straight and walked toward the windows. "Sorry, I had to recall what I've asked my past clients. And no, I've never asked anyone how they wanted to be viewed by their descendants."

"Why not? It seems a fair question."

Marietta looked out the window and down into the canal below. "Many of them fear they will not have descendants."

"Ah!" He said with a lightness that gave relief to Marietta. "Superstition. To imagine having descendants is to curse your family. It is too much pride. But here in Venice, we are ruled by a doge and a council, not a Pope. But still, we are a people rich with tradition, are we not?"

"And there are many churches," Marietta added.

"That is only to keep artists employed. For what is humanity without art?"

"Some might say art is a way to tell stories to those who cannot read," she said and smiled at him.

"You are bold. I like you. And you are looking for your easel, I presume?" He sighed and walked toward the door. "I'll have my man bring it in."

Marietta had asked one of the studio errand boys to bring an easel to the house the day before. She had always traveled to client homes with her father or another experienced artist, and between the two of them, the easel and supplies could be carried. But today, she was alone, and her arms already felt fatigued from her twenty-minute journey across Venice. If she had to also carry an easel strapped to her back, she probably wouldn't have made it across the Rialto bridge.

"Thank you, Bernardi," the man said as the servant set the easel in the center of the room. "Where would you like me?"

She stood by the windows and looked at the room to see where the light fell. Her eyes kept returning to the long, elegantly carved bench. It was morning and the light currently fell on the bookshelves opposite the bench, but in the afternoon, it would fall on the bench. If she made future visits for further studies, it would be in the afternoon, and the light would be on the bench.

"I agree with you. It is a favorite spot of mine," he said.

She looked up to see him already walking to the end of the bench furthest from the window. She asked, "Is there enough light for you to read by at this hour?"

"My eyes are not so old as all that. No, no, the morning light will suffice. Less glare. Besides, it's far brighter than a ship's quarters."

"Were you in the battle of Lepanto?"

"Weren't we all?"

Both her father and his friend, Paolo Veronese, had been commissioned for paintings of the battle of Lepanto, Venice's victory over the Turks in 1571, for power over the trade routes of the Eastern Mediterranean. Her father's mural had been destroyed in 1577 during a tragic fire in the Doge's palace. But Veronese's painting had survived. She liked Veronese's painting better than her father's, but she vowed to never admit it.

"I saw your master's mural of the battle at the palace. It was very... how shall I say?"

"Confusing?" Marietta offered.

"Yes." He smiled at her and settled into the corner of the bench. His hand found the front of the curved arm. The wood looked well polished, as if his cloak was frequently laid upon it. He continued, "But battle is confusing. I believe your master captured the spirit of Lepanto. It was a victorious day, but not a good day. Is that not the essence of confusion?"

Marietta adjusted her easel to face him, but not block the light, even though the light was currently hitting the opposite wall, there was a soft glow on the man she wished to preserve. "Do you remember much of the battle?"

"Every moment, unfortunately. I remember that one day better than all the days I knew my son."

Marietta looked around the room for any family portraits. But there were none.

"There is a portrait, if that is what you are looking for. It is in my bedroom."

"I'm dearly sorry. How old was he?"

"Only five. I left my pregnant wife to fend for herself as I went off to battle with an army of men. Then in 1577…"

She started to draw the man, sitting in his dim corner, with his hand gripped around the end of the bench arm. He squeezed and loosened his grip. Marietta wanted to put him at ease, so she talked. "The plague killed everyone in the household next to ours. I was seventeen years old. Several of the apprentices I trained with at the studio lost their parents. The Master made sure we all ate food every day. One boy, he was younger than me, I think only twelve at the time, he refused to go home. He claimed that his house was haunted by the ghosts of his dead family."

"Ah, yes." The man didn't look up at her, but tilted his head in thought. "I think it is always worse for those who survive. That is why I believe churches are designed as art galleries, and not as places of worship. For why would any God ever wish so much death upon any of its creations? Any such God is not worthy of worship. But art, now that is something to preserve and cherish."

The man's book remained closed in his hand and sat undisturbed in his lap. Marietta and the man talked about art for the next few hours. The servant brought them lunch near 1 pm, when the light was finally starting to lean toward the bench. Afterward, the man stood and walked toward the door. "Come."

She followed him down the dark hallway, into a brightly lit kitchen, and up a staircase. The length of the upper hall was lined with four windows and had five doors. He walked to the end and opened the door for her. "Come. This is my room. You wanted to see my son."

It was the room directly over the library, with two windows on one wall. Above the fireplace was a portrait of a fair-haired woman sitting on the same bench with a young boy, also fair-haired, perhaps four years old, standing next to her with his small hand on her shoulder. He had an eager expression, like he had been promised a chilled sugar-cream if he stood still long enough for his likeness to be captured.

"They are both handsome. I think you are right to hang them here. Do they bring you peace at night? Do you dream of them?"

"Yes. Yes I do. Often. My wife and I used to debate. She had a wonderful intellect. She was very practical, mind you, and not distracted by her studies. But she loved to study and challenge me. And my son, if he had grown, would have been an excellent debater in the Council of Ten. Maybe even doge one day."

"Doge?"

"Oh yes! Even at five years old, he could persuade his tutor to delay his indoor studies in favor of outdoor exercise. He would have been a talented diplomat and master of rhetoric."

An image filled Marietta's head. It was the woman's face from the bridge that morning. The woman who smeared lard on Marietta's head to keep her wig in place against the wind. The curve of the woman's chin, the plain, bulbous eyes, the cheekbones that simply formed the face, but were not prominent. The woman had such basic features, they could be used for every woman or every man. And she saw these same features in the keen expression of the small boy above the fireplace. She had an idea.

"Will you permit me some freedom with your portrait?"

The man tilted his head and leaned forward. He took a step back and looked at Marietta, then the painting, and then Marietta again.

"I do not want a portrait with my wife."

"No, but how about a portrait with your son?" Marietta looked at the man. She felt her chest and cheeks warming. "He'd be twelve now, correct?"

The man nodded. He brought his hands together, tapped his lips with his two index fingers, and then stroked his beard with one hand.

"Come, come," she said. "The light is good." The other reason for leaving so quickly was that standing in the sun of the bedroom had caused her lard-laden head to smell a bit foul, like the drippings of a tallow candle.

Marietta rushed the man back to the library and onto his bench. Her early sketch work was already complete. Now she took the values, the light and the darks, as the sun hit his cloak, face, and his hand on the arm of the bench. She noted what was in shadow and what was not. Then she loosely sketched another figure standing next to him. She saw in her mind where the same light would shine or shadow on this new figure. An hour later, she started packing her supplies.

"Can you come to the studio in two weeks?"

"Two weeks?" The man said. "Can you be done that quickly?"

"I wish you to see it before it is finished and before my master can say anything against it."

"Would he?"

"I don't know. It is something new. And he is a man who honors the old ways of Michelangelo and Titian."

"Well, you have me most intrigued. I look forward to an early viewing in two weeks."

～

MARIETTA WORKED like her father always did, at a furious pace with broad brushstrokes. She had painted four entire canvases in as many days before she settled on the composition. Then a miracle happened. A whisper echoed up to Marietta's easel.

"Robusti I think he said his name was."

"Ma'am?" said one of the young boys in the studio.

"A young man with a canvas and paints told me to come to Tintoretto's studio and ask for Robusti."

Marietta ran downstairs from the loft where she had been working. It was her. It was the Mistress of the Lard.

"You *are* a woman," the lard mistress said. "On the bridge, when your wig flapped in the wind, I thought you were a woman, but I wasn't sure if you were hiding that from the other artists."

The young boy walked away and sighed.

Marietta laughed and flicked her long, fair hair off her shoulder. "Jacopo Tintoretto is my father. Everyone here knows I was born the wrong gender. But the clients don't." Marietta approached the woman and clasped her hands. "I am so excited you've come. I have a job for you. I need you to pose for me. I will pay you. How much time are you available this week?"

The lard mistress's eyes grew large. She looked around. "This *is* the famous art studio of Tintoretto? I have been in Madonna dell'Orto. It is his paintings that cover the church, correct?"

"Yes! You are a patron of the arts. That's wonderful."

"And you want to pay me to pose for you. For what?"

"For a painting? Will you wear a wig?"

The woman freed her hands and stepped backward. Her eyes fell on the platform in the corner where four artists painted a woman, who stood nude, leaning on a chair. "What else will I be allowed to wear?"

Marietta followed the woman's gaze and laughed again. "You will be fully clothed. In fact, you might be hot. I need you to wear a long, black velvet cloak. The fabric is very difficult to capture."

"A cloak and a wig?"

"Yes, I need to paint a twelve-year-old boy."

91

"But I'm a thirty-year-old woman?"

"And I'm an artist."

MARIETTA HAD BEEN successful at hiding the canvas of the gentleman and his son from her father. Every night she covered it and slid it between several other practice canvases in her collection. Two weeks after first meeting the man in his palazzo, he arrived at the studio. Marietta was waiting for him near the studio entrance, enjoying a fresh roll and coffee with her new friend Veronica, who now made it a habit of posing for Marietta every morning.

"The drawing of Michelangelo and the color of Titian. I like it." The gentleman pointed up at the carved stone over the studio's entrance.

"My lord, welcome." Marietta was once again dressed as a man. "Come with me. The master will arrive soon and I prefer you see the portrait before he does. Oh, excuse me. My apologies. Would you like a roll or some coffee?" She asked, while still walking across the studio. The gentleman, never losing a step behind her, nodded. "Veronica, quick, would you please fetch an extra roll and coffee? Thank you."

Marietta rushed him up the stairs and into the loft. The painting was already set upon the easel but covered with a cloth. The gentleman stood in front of it with much of the same eager expression that his five-year-old son had shown in the bedroom portrait. "My master has not yet seen this, so if you object to it, please tell me and I will paint you a portrait more to your liking."

"I feel as if I'm participating in a political intrigue," he said.

Veronica arrived with a roll and coffee and set it down on a paint table behind the gentleman. Marietta looked at Veronica who clapped her hands together in a small prayer. Marietta smiled at her and pulled away the cloth.

"Oh!" The gentleman took a step toward the painting. "But how? It is him, but now. I mean..." He took a step backward and his hands felt behind himself into the empty air. Veronica grabbed a chair and slid it behind the man to catch him. His hand touched the chair, and he sat without looking, his eyes mesmerized by the canvas. "It is my son, talking to me, debating with me. And he is so bright. Look at his face. He is accepting my ideas and making them new. It is a perfect union of the wisdom of age and the movement of youth."

Marietta whispered, "Do you like it?"

"It is remarkable."

Footsteps echoed on the wooden stairs leading up to the loft. "My Lord," said Jacopo Tintoretto. "I'm glad my assistant is taking good care of you. What do you think? Are you pleased with our progress?"

Veronica offered the gentleman the roll and coffee, but he waved it away. Tintoretto took it and ate it. Then he studied the painting. His face contorted into a frown and furrowed brow. He looked back at the gentleman, but the gentleman was now staring at Veronica.

"It is you?" The gentleman asked Veronica.

"Excuse me?"

"It is you, in the painting. It is your face."

Veronica flushed and looked down. Marietta stood next to her and said, "She is a model for the studio. She reminded me of your son, so I adapted her for the painting."

Tintoretto quietly said, "I did not know you had a son?"

The gentleman could not take his eyes off Veronica. "He died in the plague." He faced the painting again. "But here, you can see that your assistant has brought him back to life for me. Here we are together, debating Aristotle's Poetics. Is it not remarkable?"

"Yes, yes, it's very good," Tintoretto said, giving his daughter a stern look. "It's not finished yet, obviously."

"I want another portrait, in six years' time. When he's a grown man, near eighteen, and soon to start his life." The gentleman faced Marietta. "Can you do that for me? Can you promise you will paint him for me?"

Marietta nodded.

The gentleman continued, "Thank you. You have given me my son. It is more than I could ever wish for. It is hope for a future that I thought was gone." He then turned back to Veronica. "Thank you. You have embodied his spirit. I hope this is not the last time we meet."

Veronica stood straighter and taller and gave a tense smile. "I'm always here in the mornings."

"Good," the gentleman said and nodded in a distracted manner. "That is good." He looked at the canvas one last time and then pulled the cloth back over it. "I look forward to the finished painting. You must all be there with me when I hang it. I insist. You will all join me for dinner."

Two months later, Marietta, dressed as an awkward man, Veronica, dressed as an elegant female, Tintoretto, dressed in unstained velvet, and the gentleman, all dined together. The portrait of the gentleman debating with his young son was ceremoniously hung in the library. Bernardi, the servant, gasped and left the room. "He was a second father to my son," the gentleman explained. "Don't worry. He likes it. He needs a moment to calm himself. I told him about it when I first returned from the studio and he has been quite earnest to see it."

To Tintoretto and Marietta's surprise, Veronica demonstrated a love of life that captured the heart of the gentleman. He vowed to teach her to read, and during their tutoring sessions, a great affection grew between them. Being only ten years her senior and very wealthy, no one in her family objected to the marriage. A year later, they had their first daughter. Two years after that, they had their first son. Two more children followed. Marietta painted all their portraits. In 1590, the gentleman commissioned Marietta to paint the second portrait of himself with his first son, who, if alive, would now be eighteen years old. But there was a problem.

"Marietta, you are pregnant." Tintoretto calmly explained to his daughter. "You cannot dress up as a man to take his portrait."

"But he commissioned it six years ago. I promised him. And if anyone would accept the idea of a female artist, it is him. He married the female model for his son's portrait."

"Women are not permitted to work independently as artists. It is vulgar. You cannot study the naked male form. The studio would be closed."

"Closed for what, Father? Why? It's 1590. The Spanish Inquisition is a faded memory." She started cleaning paint off her brushes. "I'll talk to Veronica. Maybe she'll have an idea."

Veronica had a wonderful idea. She told her husband that his favorite artist was a woman, and he said, "Of course she is. Doesn't Tintoretto know?"

When Marietta arrived, with her bulging belly and paintbrushes, the gentleman greeted her with grace and warmth. Veronica filled every food craving and made sure Marietta was comfortable. At the end of the day, the gentleman asked Marietta if she would do him a favor.

"Would you please sign your painting? The portrait in the library. Would you sign it with your name, your real name? And this next piece too?"

Marietta drew her hand to her mouth and walked to the window. She stood there, still, simply trying to breathe, as breathing had suddenly become difficult. When she turned to face her dear friend Veronica and the kind, wise gentleman, tears streamed down her cheeks. She crossed to her easel, picked up a medium-sized paintbrush, dipped it in deep blue paint, and with quick brush strokes against the dark background signed, *M. Robusti.*

INSPIRATION FOR THE
PREGNANT MAN

*M*arietta Robusti died from childbirth in 1590, at the age of thirty-six, leaving several unfinished canvases. She had three younger brothers and four younger sisters, several of whom worked in their father's, Tintoretto's, studio. Female artists during the Renaissance—Yes, there were several—often dressed as men to hide their gender, as it was inappropriate for a woman to study the naked male form. The art historian Giorgio Vasari, wrote about his contemporary, a female artist, the 16th century Florentine Dominican nun, Plautilla Nelli, that she "would have done marvelous things if, like men, she had been able to study and to devote herself to drawing and copying living and natural things." Nelli's restored 21-foot-long canvas of *The Last Supper* is displayed in Florence in the museum of Santa Maria Novella Church. It's fabulous! I actually like it better than Da Vinci's *Last Supper* in Milan.

During the Renaissance, women were not considered citizens, but property of their father, then their husband upon marriage. Thus, women could not earn a living as a professional artist because they could not write invoices. However, a convent could be paid for commissions and services, so Plautilla Nelli ran an all female art studio.

Marietta was her father's most accomplished assistant, and the number of works produced from Tintoretto's studio greatly decreased after her death. It will never be known the number of paintings produced by Marietta that are now attributed to Tintoretto. However, the painting entitled *Portrait of Two Men*, the painting upon which I based this story, is signed by MR and thought to be Marietta Robusti's only surviving signed work. It hangs in the Gemaldegalerie Alte Meister in Dresden, Germany.

Other canvases now thought to be painted by Marietta are:

Old Man and Boy, Kunsthistorisches Museum, Vienna

Portrait of Ottavio Strada, Rijksmuseum, Amsterdam

Head of Man, After the Antique, a drawing sold at Christie's in Paris in 2021 for €100,000. Scrawled across the drawing are the words "this head is by the hand of modanna Marietta," hypothesized to be added by her father to distinguish the drawing from others in his studio. The drawing depicts the Roman emperor Vitellius, and is based on a copy of a bust Tintoretto kept in his workshop.

Marietta's talents were not completely forgotten and at least two biographers commented on her. "Marietta had a brilliant mind like her father. She painted such works that men were astonished by her talent," writes Carlo Ridolfi, author of a biography of Jacopo Tintoretto and two of his children, Domenico and Marietta, first published in 1642. According to Ridolfi, Marietta dressed as a boy in order to assist her father on his projects and produced works of her own invention. Raffaello Borghini, a contemporary of Tintoretto's reported that Marietta was requested as a court artist by the Holy Roman Emperor Maximilian II, Archduke Ferdinand of Austria, and King Philip II of Spain. However, "Greatly loving his daughter, [Tintoretto] did not want her taken from his sight," writes Borghini.

The Venetian Renaissance master, Jacopo Robusti, known as Tintoretto, is buried in Madonna dell'Orto in Venice next to his favorite daughter nicknamed, "La Tintoretta." His house, where he lived from 1574 until his death in 1594, can be viewed at No. 3399 Fondamenta dei Mori. It has a plaque remembering Tintoretto, and the facade features a small statue of Hercules with a club.

No power in death can tear our names apart,
As none in life could rend thee from my heart.
Yes, Leonora! it shall be our fate
To be entwined for ever—but too late!

Lord Byron
The Lament of Tasso
Published July 17, 1817

THE HAUNTED PALAZZO

*P*resent day
Venice, Italy
An Alexis Lynn adventure from *Will Write for Wine.*

IT'S NEVER RECOMMENDED to sleep alone in a six-hundred-year-old haunted Venetian palazzo. So I didn't. I took a friend with endless curls of boisterous red hair and my dog, a scrappy little black and grey terrier named Toto. It was late February, and the air was moist, cold, and fetid inside the old palazzo. Despite the offensive smell, it wasn't all spider webs and rough wood. My friend Claudio and his architectural restoration company had already spent nine months modernizing the palazzo with new electrical wiring, wood paneling, tiling, marble counters, bathrooms with actual plumbing instead of a chamber pot, and refurbishing the original grand staircase, which required a stonemason. Apparently in Venice, one can make a living as a stonemason. Claudio told me that several of his workmen believed the palazzo to be haunted, which would not be unusual in the creepy, fog-laden city of Venice.

Claudio didn't believe in ghosts. Many native Venetians didn't. I think Venetians built a mental block toward all legends, myths, and ghosts in order to retain their mental health in what was obviously a haunted city. I'd only lived in Venice for seven weeks, so ghosts, devils, murderous neighbors, tortured monks who wreaked havoc on the plumbing, and legends of broken-hearted witches seeking revenge, all remained glorious to me.

The palazzo's only tragic history we knew about it was a Romeo and Juliet-style story from around 1600. A son from an enemy family across the Grand Canal fell in love with the daughter of the palazzo's family, and both their lives ended tragically when their secret marriage was discovered. Why Claudio cared if the palazzo was haunted or not was because a fourth-floor bedroom kept seeping water from the wall around the window, but the source of the water couldn't be discovered. If a ghost was causing the water damage, Claudio wanted me to convince the ghost to move out, or move on, or simply vanquish it. I repeat, Claudio didn't believe in ghosts, but he could find no other explanation for the water leak.

How I was going to persuade a ghost to do anything, I had no idea. I had never talked to a ghost. Claudio had heard from his cousin that I had sensed the ghosts of a long-ago sword battle in her wine vault, and a pool of blood seeped up through the floor afterward. I think it was just a wet iron deposit below the stone floor, but now Claudio and most of the Gandolfi and Veron family members all believed I could solve their ghostly problems. I apparently had ghost-talking superpowers. Lucky me!

I couldn't find a sleeping bag to borrow from anyone, as camping wasn't a popular activity among Venetians. I packed some blankets, a pillow, a bottle of wine, a second bottle of wine, and some snacks for me, Toto, and my friend Jennifer with the big red hair. Jen had never seen, met, nor ever felt a ghost. However, at the age of fifty-two, she admitted to being open-minded that ghosts might exist. "And I live in a house from the 1920s, thus I'm hoping there might be some flapper ghosts hanging around just waiting to party with me. Besides," Jen said, "As I get older, the idea of an afterlife becomes more and more appealing."

We settled into the problematic fourth-floor bedroom with the canal-view window that mysteriously seeped water. I hoped to enjoy a glorious sunset from our upper view, but the gloomy winter sky dominated the bell towers of Venice. I turned on our battery-powered lantern. The palazzo had working electricity, but I doubted a ghost would make an appearance under the glow of modern lighting. Claudio had discouraged candles since much of the house had flammable chemicals lying around for the restoration work, including this bedroom which had a mural soon to be restored by my husband.

Jen and I both wrote historical fiction because we loved to geek out on history, so sleeping in an ancient palazzo waiting for a ghost to present a historical mystery to us, totally scratched our Nancy-Drew-meets-Sherlock-Holmes-set-in-Renaissance-Venice inner child.

The room echoed with our footsteps and movements. It was long and narrow, with the one large window opposite the door and all the other walls were interior. Jen was tall, nearly six feet, so I guessed the ceiling to be about eight feet tall, which was short compared to the other floors below containing the salons, dining, library, and study, but normal for an upper bedroom floor. The wall mural depicted a city scene of Venice with a large church and a campo. I didn't recognize it, which meant it was in the Dorsoduro, probably somewhere near this palazzo. I had memorized most of Venice by now, but I hadn't methodically explored the Dorsoduro area, aside from the Accademia gallery. I enjoyed the challenge of proving that every printed map, and I mean every single map, guidebook, and hotel pamphlet of Venice, contained inaccuracies. I also enjoyed not getting lost when I took Toto for a walk. That being said, getting lost in Venice is a grand way to spend an evening.

Another grand way to spend an evening is hanging out in an ancient palazzo, waiting for a ghost to appear and dampen a windowsill. Jen and I examined the windowsill. It was currently dry, but a clear outline of a U-shaped paint discoloration could be seen on the wall below the windowsill. It had all been recently replastered, restored, and repainted, yet the water stains appeared fresh. I could see why Claudio was irritated. In Italian, he had ranted to me, "That section of the room was completely covered in dampness and mold, and four patch jobs later, the water continues to seep through. I can't find a source. This project is supposed to end in another two months, but I don't know what to do with that wall."

Jen had restored her historic 1920s home in Denver and I'd suffered three condo renovations, so we both knew a bit about construction. We hypothesized various water sources, like a poorly designed gutter system, a leak in the six-hundred-year-old roof, porous stones hollowing out a trail to this window, or really angry birds carrying up water from the narrow canal below. We weren't ruling out the angry bird hypothesis. The wind patterns between the *calles* and bell towers had a way of disorienting all small flying objects. It was funny to watch a bird enter a campo and visibly relax. Birds sat in Venetian campos far longer than any other place on the planet. This palazzo was nowhere near a campo or any large open space. It sat on a narrow canal at the corner of two narrow *calles* and had an interior courtyard. Birds flying in through an open window had been a problem during the renovations. The birds and the rain were the main reason most of the windows had been closed and the air smelled stale and fetid. Restoration chemicals, such as turpentine, didn't help either. But since the windows had been mostly closed for two months, as much as we loved the angry bird hypothesis, we had to conclude something else was probably dampening the windowsill and wall.

Jen wrinkled her nose and said, "If we get high on the chemical smell, do you think it will be easier to talk to the ghost?"

"Absolutely!" I said as I unscrewed the twist top on our first wine bottle and poured two glasses. Jen and I had decided to take the night off from writing and brought a book with us to read out loud, *Venetian Legends and Ghost Stories, A Guide to Places of Mystery in Venice*. It was a guidebook filled with ghost stories about locations you passed during a walking tour of Venice. It was written in 2000 by a Murano islander and native Venetian, but I'd found an English language copy in my favorite pet store/coffee bar/book seller combo shop. We read the

Dorsoduro section hoping to learn something about this palazzo, but there was nothing. However, we did learn that pretty much everyone who had owned or lived in Ca' Dario, a neighboring palazzo, had died in some gruesome, horrible way. Fascinating!

We had just started reading about the Castello area when the room suddenly became cold.

"Jen, do you feel that?"

Toto stood up and climbed on my lap, trying to cuddle into my blanket.

"It's freezing," she said. "Oh my gosh. Look at my breath." She attempted to blow smoke rings and started making fog clouds in the air.

We sat very still and watched and listened. We both tensed at the same time. We heard someone weeping. Toto barked. I shushed him and held him tightly. We heard mumbling in Italian or Venetian, and sobbing, extreme sobbing, with hitched breaths and chest heaves.

"She's mumbling something," I said.

"Do you understand what she's saying?" Jen asked. Toto started to squirm.

"Something about a letter. And a church. Quiet." Jen and I both listened intently. The mumbling and sobbing seemed to come from outside the room. Toto escaped my arms and ran toward the door and froze. Then he laid down and whimpered. I ran to the open bedroom door, picked up Toto, and looked down the hallway.

The hair on my arms stood straight up. I physically shivered. A girl in full Venetian Renaissance dress stood only six feet from me. She looked directly at me and shouted, "No!"

I ran back to Jen. The ghost followed me and entered the room. She paced in front of the mural and continued mumbling and sobbing.

"She's still talking about a letter and a church," I said. "And Christ. And a saint. I think she's praying. Is that Latin?"

Toto was intently focused on the ghost and watched it pace, his little head moving back and forth while I held him.

"Yep. That's Latin. She's praying," I said.

Jen looked at me and asked, "Should we try to get her attention?"

"It's an angry ghost. I'm perfectly happy for her to ignore us," I said, but before I could finish my sentence, Jen threw a cracker toward the door. It flew through the ghost and fell to the ground. Toto wriggled loose from me and dove for the cracker. Ghost or no ghost, there was food on the floor. The ghost jumped as Toto ran through her. She stopped pacing and stared at my dog. My spine tingled, and I feared for Toto. I shouted at the ghost, but she made no notice of me. I shouted, "Toto come!" But he only crouched down and whimpered. The air grew more intense, like it was charged with electricity. I ran to Toto and scooped him up in my arms again. My right arm felt like electricity had surged through it.

"Alexis," Jen said, "Can she see you?"

The ghost stared directly at me. I reached out my right hand and tried to touch her. Electricity surged through my hand. "She's pure energy," I told Jen. "If another energy source passes through her, it disrupts her particles."

Jen laughed at me. "Are you using quantum physics to explain ghosts?"

"No," I smirked. "But touch her. It feels really weird. Like an electrical storm. Doesn't the air in Denver feel like this, this room, before a big electrical storm?"

Jen raised her wine glass. "Offer her some wine." I wondered if Jen was drunk, or perhaps she thought she was drunk because she was witnessing a ghost for the first time in her life. Anyone's first ghost is a bit traumatizing.

The ghost stared at me more intensely. She had long brown hair pulled back in a bun with tendrils from the side of her head hanging down. They looked like they had been styled as ringlets, but had gotten damp. I looked at her dress. It was clearly dry but made of thick fabric, velvets, and stitched brocade. It might be damp and I wouldn't notice. But it was not dripping water. Her cheeks were flushed and her breathing rapid, which made me think she had just come in from outside and raced up four flights of stairs.

"Can you hear me?" I asked the ghost.

There was no response or reaction. I passed my hand through her arm again, and she pulled her arm away and looked around. She could respond to my energy, but didn't know where it was coming from.

She stopped turning around and placed a hand on the wall mural. She touched the bell tower of the church in the painting, then kissed it.

"Jen, do you know what church that is?"

"Um, San Trovaso, I think. Yep, it has two facades. It's quite lovely inside. Very tall. There are some Tintorettos."

Toto barked and his head followed the ghost as she ran to the window, still mumbling in Italian. Toto started whimpering again. The ghost leaned out the closed window and looked downward. Was she waiting for a boat? I handed Toto to Jen and rushed to the window, opened it, and leaned out. The view only showed the dark, hushed water below.

The ghost spoke in Latin again. Praying. She closed her eyes and climbed into the window, swinging her legs over the edge, her heavy skirts draping down the windowsill and ledge. Then she pushed herself out.

I gulped. Even though I saw it coming, I still wasn't expecting it. I leaned out and watched her fall and disappear as she hit the water. The water didn't ripple or move with her entry. She just vanished beneath the surface. I grabbed the window and closed it.

"Holy crap! Do you think a fall like that killed her?" I asked Jen who still sat in the center of the room, holding Toto, and sipping her wine glass. Toto squirmed away and put his paws on the windowsill.

Jen shrugged and said, "Maybe. We're about 40-50 feet high. How deep is the water? Did she hit anything on the way down? Could she swim? Would her clothes cause her to drown?"

We hypothesized for several minutes while cuddling with a very stressed Toto.

"Jen, Toto's paws are wet." I ran to the windowsill and sure enough, it was wet. "Look, it's in the shape of her skirts when she sat on the window just before she jumped. Her skirts must have been wet. Really wet. The ghost really is the cause of the water leak. But why are her skirts wet? Why?"

Jen stood up while still holding her wine glass, which was an interesting display of her yoga skills, and examined the windowsill with me. "Are you suggesting that if we can stop the ghost lady from getting her skirts wet, thus she might perform a dry-skirted suicide, then the windowsill will no longer get moldy?"

"That's brilliant! Yes. We can't talk to her, so we're probably not going to prevent her from committing suicide. But if we can prevent her from getting her skirts wet, then we solve Claudio's problem."

"This whole scenario is a great concept for a television show," Jen said. Jen wrote novels, but several of her friends were screenwriters and they had been encouraging her to pitch her books and other ideas as television shows. She hadn't had any success yet, but her ideas were great!

"It would need to be a comedy, and death is rarely funny."

Jen started pacing and said, "That's the challenge." She continued pacing while staring at the mural on the wall.

"Why do you think she kissed the bell tower?" I asked.

"It's probably where she kissed her lover."

Jen started pacing faster and then stopped. Toto barked. "You said it was a Romeo and Juliet story, right?" I nodded. "San Trovaso, this church," she pointed to the church in the mural with the bell tower, "see here, this church has two identical facades. What did our little haunted guidebook just say about this?" She reached for the book and flipped to the required section.

IN THE PAST, *the church was neutral ground for the nicolotti and the castellani. In case of a marriage between two young members of the opposing factions, the castellans entered through the southern portal and the nicolotti from the portal facing the canal.*

"But," I said, "the family name for this palazzo was never Nicolotti or Castellani? Claudio said the various family names from the past centuries. I can't remember them, but Nicolotti and Castellani don't sound familiar."

"It's in lower case in the guidebook. It's not a family name, it's a faction; like republican or democrat. I remember reading about these two factions. The castellani resided in the castello and the nicolotti were on this side of the Grand Canal. It probably had something to do with dock or port rights and custom houses. Who knows?" Jen drank more wine. "So this girl secretly married a boy from the other faction. Oh! Maybe they got married in the bell tower. Her father finds out, forbids her to ever see him again, and she commits suicide." Jen clapped her hands in triumph. Then her face collapsed. "So why is her skirt wet?"

"I thought the rest of her looked damp, but not sodden enough to leave water on a windowsill. But the material was such a heavy velvet that I wouldn't notice if it was wet. What did you see?"

"Um, she was more like a shimmer in the air to me. But I could hear her, sort of. Maybe. To be honest, if you hadn't been standing right next to her, and Toto hadn't been barking at her, I probably wouldn't have even noticed her."

"She was crystal clear to me. I could draw you the pattern of her gold brocade stitching. How come you couldn't see her? That's interesting." I wanted to ponder this for a moment, but my head was too entangled with the mystery. "Anyway, her skirt must have been wet, but I don't think all of her was, just the bottom hem of her skirt. How would she get the bottom hem wet?"

"*Acqua alta?*" Jen said.

"Oh! Did they have high waters in 1600? I bet they did. That's an interesting idea. What else? Getting in and out of a boat. Getting splashed in the kitchens or at the well in the courtyard? What about the water landing?" I walked back to the window, opened it, and leaned out again. "This palazzo has a water entrance. A boat could have approached and splashed her with its wake." I closed the window again. "Let's go down and check it out."

Jen, Toto, and I trotted down four flights, flipping on the staircase lights as we descended. The water entrance of the palazzo was in a stone room with a gate and a new inset door that looked like aged wood. Curious, I tapped on it. "I think it's fiberglass or PVC. Smart! It won't rot." However, the door in the wall to the right of us was completely rotted at the bottom. There was an ancient, rusted latch and an old lock on the door, like something you might find on an old treasure chest from a pirate ship. "What do you think is in there?"

"The dungeon!" Jennifer said with sudden glee.

"Or it's probably just a larder for groceries."

"No," Jennifer said as she walked over to it. "It's the dungeon. Claudio told me this place had a dungeon, but the new owners had to cut costs, so Claudio isn't being paid to renovate it."

"That's cool! I want to see a Venetian dungeon."

Jen, who was a bit of a yoga queen and oddly strong, handed me her wine glass.

"You carried this four flights without spilling it?"

Jen laughed, "We all have our talents." She walked up to the ancient door, grabbed the lock, and clanked it against the latch. Nothing happened. She pulled down on the lock, but it didn't come open. She yanked it again, and the latch broke. A large U-shaped chunk of metal with the lock attached crashed to the ground. Toto jumped away. "Whoops," Jen said and laughed. "I meant to simply pop the old lock open so we could close it again. I didn't mean to break off the entire attachment."

"Will Claudio be mad at us?"

"Probably. That means we'll have great make-up sex."

I forgot to mention that Jen was currently sleeping with Claudio.

The ancient wooden door had swelled to fill its stone-arched frame. Jen tried to lift and jostle it loose, but it wouldn't budge. "How badly do you want to see the dungeon?" she asked me.

"Do you think it could help solve our ghost mystery?" I said with a smirk.

"Of course!" she said to me with another smirk. "I think it's entirely necessary that we investigate—investigate being the operative word—that we investigate the dungeon of a fifteenth century palazzo for clues as to why a ghost has wet skirts."

"And honestly, when will we ever again have the opportunity to see an ancient palazzo dungeon, especially one that hasn't been opened or entered for at least a generation or two or three?" I examined the swollen wood of the door around the stone. The wood had actually grown over the edges of the stone arch like fingers gripping into stony flesh. "Jen, I don't think this door has been opened for centuries."

"This is totally amazing, isn't it?" Jen said, with a mischievous gleam in her eye and a bounce in her red curls. We were both historical nuts, so this was a bit dreamy, in a gothic, horror sort of way. "I'll be right back," she said as she headed toward the stairs. "I saw a tool chest on the next floor."

What was she going to do? Saw through the door? "No power tools!" I shouted up the staircase. Toto watched her run up the stairs, but stayed with me, sniffed the door and wagged his tail. He was also curious. I dug into my pocket and produced a salmon treat for him.

Jen returned with a flat pry bar.

"Hey," I said, "That's what I used to remove awful tack boards from carpeting. I hate carpet. Why do people still use carpet? I think everyone needs to remove a room of carpeting so they can see how gross it is, with all the mouse droppings, dead termites, flea powder, dead skin flakes, and lord knows what else, then no one would ever again install carpeting."

Jen held up her pry bar/carpet-tack-board-removal tool and said, "It can also open pickle jars and slice wedged potatoes. This tool should be introduced in elementary school. Start them young, I always say. Fire up the imagination!"

"Precisely!" I picked up Toto, just in case the door fell down.

Jen slipped the skinny edge of the pry bar between the wood and the stone frame and worked her way around the entire door. She gave the handle a good tug, and miracle of miracles, it swung open. I applauded while holding Toto, which was a bit awkward. My claps echoed into the new room. That was creepy.

Jen pulled her phone from her back pocket and flipped on the flashlight. I did the same. The room was simply a room, with no windows, but our view was narrow. we needed to enter and walk past a six-foot-long wall in order to view the rest of the room. At this point, there was no staircase descending into a dungeon, because well, it was Venice, and rooms below the water level were rare. The floor of the room was the same level we stood on now. Toto whimpered.

"Toto doesn't like that room," I said.

"It smells funky," Jen said. "Like rotten fish in a donut fryer and then cleaned with vinegar."

"Is that from personal experience?"

"Teenage children do strange things," she said and gave me an eye roll. She looked around for something. I handed Jen her wine glass. "*Grazie.*" She took a deep swig. "Should we enter? I'm feeling kind of tingly about this. And not in a good way." She set her wine glass on the floor just beyond the door and adjusted her grip on the pry bar.

"Phone light in one hand and a weapon in the other. Good strategy," I said.

She looked at me. "Is Toto your weapon?"

Toto cocked his head and looked up at me. I hugged him and whispered that I had no intention of using him as a weapon.

"Do you hear water dripping?" Jen asked. We entered, Jen in front, and me following. She got to the end of the wall and peeked around with her phone light. "Mother of pearl!"

"What?" I tried to peek around her. She stepped farther in, and down, and I shined my light on the room. In front of us, a narrow swath of floor descended a stone ramp about two feet down. The floor we stood on was the same level as the entrance floor, but the rest of the room, surrounding the lowered ramped floor, was built up a foot higher. The raised sides were lined with crates. At the end of the dropped floor was an arched ceiling with iron bars and a gate that led to an underground canal. "Do you think they were smugglers?"

Jen laughed. "Wow, this is fascinating!"

"This is low tide," I said. "That's a sewage canal. Most of the residences above have, or had in the past, old chutes for the sewage that led into underground canals."

Jen pointed her phone light at me and then redirected it back at the sewage canal. "How do you know that?"

"When you're researching one of your historical fiction books, how often do you go down a rabbit hole?"

"Point taken. Continue," she said.

"You know how when you're taking a boat down one of the side canals of Venice and you see long, low arches peeking above the water a few inches? Those are sewage canals. When it's low tide, they're accessible. Sort of. Like now. This canal opening, wherever it opens, is probably a foot, maybe eighteen inches tall above the water level." I walked to the water gate and shined my light upward. "But this tunnel has a high ceiling. That might be unusual. I'm not sure. So a boat waits until low tide, drifts under the low arch, and then enters a high ceilinged tunnel where the boat crew can sit up again, docks here, out of the eyes of customs, unloads in secret, and the family can earn a greater profit on unregulated goods." I shined my phone light up and down the sewage tunnel and found a visible sewage chute directly across from our water gate. "There, see that. That's an old sewage chute. Everything now is supposed to use modern drainage pipes, so sewage is no longer dropped directly into the ocean, but Venice hasn't been fully modernized. That's why canal water is nasty. Gosh, it stinks down here. Sorry, Toto. Geez, imagine what his poor little nose is going through."

"You journeyed down quite a research rabbit hole to learn all that," Jen said.

I shined my light back on the crates. "These crates are short. They could sit on the floor of a narrow boat and glide under a low arch."

Jen examined the crates with her phone light. She said, "These crates look seriously old. Do you think this room has been locked up since the smuggling days? If that's what was happening."

"Maybe. The sewage smell is certainly concentrated down here. And it's really humid. There's been no recent airflow, but it would probably smell the same after one year or four hundred years."

We shined our lights around the room and Jen tried to open one of the top crates with her pry bar. I said, "The *acqua alta* has been as high as six feet. Even those high crates would have been completely submerged at least once or twice. Any guess at the treasures inside? *Santo Christo*—"

"Mother of pearl!"

Toto whined and squirmed. Both our phone lights focused on a skeleton in tattered, moldy clothing with a crab crawling out of its eye socket. "Holy Disney!" I said. "That is straight out of *Pirates of the Caribbean!* Whole new ball game. We're going."

We quickly retreated, closed the ancient wooden door, found a scrap of wood to use as a wedge to keep it closed, shook the icky willies off of us, and called Claudio.

Evidently, finding human remains in old palazzos was not unusual, as Claudio found no need to rush over at 2 am. Instead, he asked us to remain in the palazzo until morning, since he had locked us in and we didn't have a key. Jen fought with him and then threatened to deny him passionate make-up sex. He was there in thirty minutes to lock up behind us.

When we got back to the apartment, we turned on every possible light. Jen had just witnessed her first ghost and her first dead body, so she sat on the sofa with a full glass of wine. I feared Toto had damaged his olfactory senses as he kept wiping his nose on the floor, on the sofa, on the chairs, on his bed, and even leaped into the bathtub at one point. Toto hated the bathtub. Toto and I took a shower to get the funk of mold and sewage out of our hair.

All three of us sat on the sofa and listened to the silence of the room. Jen stared into her wine glass and said, "Ghosts are real. What if I die and I don't move on? What if I'm doomed or cursed to live the same horrible night over and over again for centuries?"

"Eventually someone will send in a human to figure out how to help you find closure. And what would you do that would warrant a horrible eternity?"

"What about the girl tonight? Our Juliet. She died of a broken heart and now lives her suicide over and over again."

Jen made me ask a question I'd never considered before. Why did someone become a ghost? Was it a punishment? Was it unfinished business? From all the stories of hauntings I'd read, and I meant eyewitness accounts, not fiction, the ghost was usually a bad person who did something bad. This made me think about our ghost tonight. Did she commit suicide because of a broken heart, or because she did something bad?

The next day, Claudio had the Venetian authorities remove the body from the sewage cellar, or as I liked to call it, the smuggler's hold. There was a legal entanglement with the crates we discovered, as the new owners technically owned everything in the palazzo, so they wanted the crates opened and inventoried. The Accademia had the crates moved to their nearby museum and unpacked. Several crates contained fine porcelain from the early 1600s. Another contained spools of silver and gold thread. All the other crates were reported to hold foodstuffs and alcohol, which had all been ruined by its long tenure in the smuggler's hold.

But Jen's concern over a future ghostly end to her life haunted me. I wanted to understand our Juliet. Was she a victim or a villain?

Once the skeleton was removed from the smuggler's hold, Juliet never reappeared again, or at least the wall below the windowsill remained dry. But who was Juliet?

Every church in Venice had amazingly thorough parish records. I had recently read an article in *Nature* that chronicled all the deaths in Venice during the plague years of 1630-31 to study the spread of plagues and compare it to modern-day pandemics. All the data came from church parish records. The museum had found manifests in the crates from August 1601, so I started my search there.

San Trovaso had a marriage record from June 2, 1601, for a Leonora Salvatici from the Castello district, to Antonio Balsimio from the Dorsoduro district. I had Claudio look up the ownership history of the palazzo and it was originally owned by the Balsimio family. I found nothing in the archives about the Balsimio family. However, if they had been smugglers, the family might have expunged all records.

I formed a hypothesis. Perhaps the castellani faction from the

Castello had discovered that the Balsimio family of the nicolotti faction in Dorsoduro was smuggling goods and avoiding customs taxes. Our Juliet's mission, young Leonora Salvatici of the warring faction, was to shut down the smuggling ring. She seduced and secretly married the son of the Balsimio family. One night, his parents are out and he invites his secret bride home with him. She asks to see the smugglers' hold. He shows it to her. She kills him and leaves his body in the hold. This is why her skirt is wet and stains the window wall, both with physical water and her guilt. She closes the door to the hold, but the parents return home and she dashes upstairs to the fourth-floor bedroom with the wall mural. She frets about killing a person she possibly loved—she did kiss the church tower in the mural —and can't live with herself. She prays and prays and finally jumps from the window to either escape arrest or commit suicide. The parents find their murdered son, possibly learn of the secret marriage to Leonora, a castellani, and out of fear of exposure to either faction, they end their smuggling ring and leave Venice. The palazzo changed owners in November 1601, only a few months later. Apparently, the new owners never bothered to see what was behind the locked door.

This hypothesis made Leonora a murderer and explained why she had to relive her suicide every night, leaving a clue behind that would lead to the discovery of her crime. Once her crime was discovered, then her guilt was released and she could move on to her eternal resting place, whatever that might be.

I explained my hypothesis to Jen a few nights later over dinner at Claudio's favorite osteria. Her fear of forever walking the earth slowly reduced with each bite of food. However, it would be hard not to relax while eating amazing squid ink cuttlefish pasta with a fabulously paired bottle of Barolo. Claudio had also informed us that the palazzo owners were required to pay a 10% finder's fee for the goods discovered and sold to the museum, which amounted to 5,000 euros for each of us. That might also have increased Jen's convivial mood. Either way, she no longer fretted about becoming a ghost and reliving her horrible death for centuries.

When I asked her if she believed in ghosts, even though she didn't fully see or hear our Juliet/Leonora, she said the most wonderful thing. Jen looked me straight in the eye and said, "You're not crazy. Ghosts exist. Whether they can be explained by physics doesn't matter. They're out there. And you can see them, feel them, and hear them. That's pretty magical."

I said, "And sometimes they stink." I told her the story of a dead Scottish laird who smoked the vilest cigars while he roamed from room to room in a Scottish castle. "The stench, randomly wafting about every few hours made it impossible to sleep." She laughed, which made me laugh. After eating squid ink pasta, we both looked like black-toothed hags, ready to challenge the witches and devils of Venice as we stumbled home down the narrow, shadow-filled *calles*.

INSPIRATION FOR THE HAUNTED
PALAZZO

*E*very palazzo in Venice has a ghost story, as does every campo, canal and calle. The book Alexis and Jennifer read while passing the time with a bottle of wine, *Venetian Legends and Ghost Stories, A Guide to Places of Mystery in Venice,* is a real book, and where I learned about the feud between the two Venetian factions of the *nicolotti* and the *castellani.*

The early sewage system of Venice described in the story is based in fact, but whether or not a sewage tunnel could be used for smuggling, is speculative.

The parish records of Venice are extremely well preserved and filled with secret marriages, which weren't so secret. The marriage and specific motivations I created for this story are fictitious, but similar scenarios occurred.

Something humorous I learned while researching this story and Venice's smelly infrastructure, is that both Edgar Allan Poe and Wilkie Collins wrote stories set in Venice, but about palazzos with extensive basements. From what I've researched, and from the many issues with flooding that Venice suffers, it would be impossible for a basement to exist. In Edgar Allan Poe's story *The Cask of Amontillado,* 1846, the two characters "passed down a long and winding staircase" below a palazzo and travel through an extensive tunnel system seeking the vault with the infamous wine cask. Poe never specifically says the story takes place in Venice, but the characters are speaking of "Italian vintages," it is during the "supreme madness of the Carnival season," and specifically uses the word, "palazzo."

In *The Haunted Hotel: A Mystery of Modern Venice*, written by Wilkie Collins in 1878, the Venetian palazzo in the story that is converted into a hotel has underground dungeons that play a prominent role in the novel. If you enjoy a good gothic ghost story, this short book is great fun. However, I doubt that any palazzo in Venice has an underground dungeon, but I haven't been in all of them, so I might be wrong. It is conceivable that a dungeon might be cut into the petrified pylons that support the buildings of Venice, but it would probably cause structural support issues and would probably flood. Everything floods in Venice.

It excites me to think about well-known authors being so enchanted with Venice that they set their stories in the magical city, but never had the opportunity to travel there. It also makes me a little sad. Poe and Collins would have loved Venice and all its glorious hauntings!

Have you ever found a basement in Venice?

"God would've made His will know without books, considering how very few could read them when Jesus of Nazareth lived, had it been His pleasure to ratify any peculiar mode of worship. As to your immortality, if people are to live, why die? And our carcases, which are to rise again, are they worth raising? I hope, if mine is, that I shall have a better pair of legs than I have moved on these two-and-twenty years, or I shall be sadly behind in the squeeze into Paradise."

Lord Byron
Letter to Francis Hodgson regarding his disbelief in religion, Sept. 13, 1811.

THE SECRET VAULT

*M*arch 1510
Soave, Italy

F<small>RANCESCO</small> C<small>ORNARO</small> <small>MARVELED</small> at the candle flame shimmering through the red and gold stripes in his Venetian wine glass. After conquering the castle of Soave, removing the imperial guards of the Holy Roman Emperor, Maximilian I, and rightfully returning the medieval fortress to the Republic of Venice, Cornaro had sent a rider forty miles home to his lagoon city. The rider returned with six perfect Venetian wine glasses, custom blown on the isle of Murano by a family employee.

Cornaro sniffed the air. It smelled sweet, with jasmine floating through the window. He admired jasmine. It was a hearty bramble that survived battles far better than people. It had taken two weeks to remove the corpses and clean the bloodstains from the stones and tapestries. Cornaro never again wanted to witness war. War created a disconnect with humanity.

His wine glass, a statement of high civilization, needed filling. He entered the salon to greet his friend, military commander, and master of Soave Castle, Paolo Gradenigo.

"Cornaro! Good man!" Paolo shouted. "Please, sit with us. We are discussing your fortunes in Cyprus. How many sugar mills does your family now own?"

Cornaro gave Paolo a quick smile and then narrowed his eyes on an unknown elderly man who appeared very relaxed upon a long padded bench.

The salon's intruder said, "I apologize. Discussing another man's fortune is an odd topic of conversation. It only came up as I was mentioning my own investments in Cyprus."

"And what are those?" Cornaro asked.

"Shipping ports, wine, a few other basics of life. Safe investments. I only trade in safe investments. My father, before his death in Bologna, always said to be safe with money and risky in love. I believe my mother was smarter than him. Is it not always a risk for a man to possess a wife with greater intellect?"

"Ha! It is the greatest risk," said Paolo with too much enthusiasm. Cornaro noticed the carafe of wine was half empty and worried that his young friend's loose tongue might reveal military secrets to this stranger. Cornaro signaled to Paolo to join him at the end of the room. Paolo, a twenty-five-year-old military man, sighed and ambled his towering frame and broad shoulders across the room. He stared down at Cornaro.

Cornaro bluntly stated, "He's a Jew."

"And we are the Republic of Venice," Paolo said with a flippant wave of his hand. "We offer safety to all Jewish refugees. And he grew up in Bologna. He's as Italian as you or me."

"We are Venetian nobility. Our great-grandfathers were Doges of Venice. Bologna is not Venice. Bologna is now a papal state."

"Abraham's none too pleased about that either. That's why he's here, in the newly, re-established, Republic of Venice. Besides, he's rich. And we're at war. Anyone at war can always use a good lender." Paolo slightly slurred his words while he refilled his wineglass.

"My family is bearing the costs of war against the Holy Roman

Emperor, so Mother Venice doesn't have to submit to the usury of his sort."

"Ha! Well, the war is costing more than all of Cyprus can provide. We need the Jews," Paolo said and sipped his wine. "You know what, Cornaro?" he asked with a slight slur on Corn-arrr-o, "I think you need to relax." Paolo filled Cornaro's wine glass. "Battle has made you wearisome. I mean worrisome. You worry. All the time. Here's what I propose. Go count some coins, drink some wine," he pushed Cornaro's glass into his hand, "wear those fancy jeweled slippers you like, and we can discuss Maximilian's troop movements in the morning. Abraham has seen his army. He might be useful. I'll interrogate him. He trusts me. Then you won't feel that the evening was a waste."

"I'm sending you to bed. No more talking." Cornaro sat down his wine glass and took away Paolo's glass.

"Have you forgotten that I am your commander?" Paolo said with sudden lucidity. He stood at his full height, tall and stiff, but still smelling of drink and his earlier horse ride.

"It is precisely that memory which implores me to protect you. Leave. I will interrogate the Jew. I agree that he may hold useful information. I applaud you for establishing trust. I will be his enemy and tomorrow he will once again confide in you."

Paolo's shoulders slumped, and his neck and jaw muscles relaxed. "I like your thinking." He reached for his glass, but Cornaro moved it away. Paolo pointed at his glass. "That's good wine. Our supply is getting low. I admire your strategic mind, but you will not instruct me to stop drinking in my own castle, when my command of it may not last another week. I will let you send me away so you may question this man, but tomorrow, you will breakfast with me."

Cornaro nodded and handed Paolo his wine glass. He motioned to two soldiers and requested they escort Paolo to his quarters.

Cornaro, at thirty-two years old, had seen and learned enough about spies and war to not trust anyone he hadn't known since childhood. He'd saved a ten-year-old Paolo from being smashed between two boats during a Venetian festival, and since then, he had always protected the fearless young boy. Paolo would one day be the head of the Gradenigo family, and possibly a Doge. A year ago, when Cornaro's father returned to Venice with the horrific news of Maximilian's fast-approaching army, the fall of the areas surrounding Milan, and the defeat of Venice's last stronghold, the fortress castle of Soave, Paolo volunteered to lead an army to retake the fortress. Six months later, in the fall of 1509, Paolo succeeded. He could play a battlefield, strategize, gain trust from his military leaders, and take a castle. However, if Cornaro asked him not to fight, Paolo couldn't comprehend the conversation. Paolo was deaf to lessons of diplomacy. Which was why Venice's governing body, the Council of Ten, asked Francesco Cornaro, son of their celebrated diplomat who gave them Cyprus, to assist the young commander, Paolo Gradenigo.

Cornaro studied the Jew from across the room. The Jew studied Cornaro.

The Jew finally lifted his glass of wine, drank, and broke the stand-off by gesturing for Cornaro to take a seat. He said, "I have come to expect suspicion. Please, tension is thick enough outside of these walls, let us be civil within them."

Cornaro nodded. He smoothed his tunic, adjusted his small black velvet cap, picked up his wine glass, and approached. He sat on the edge of his favorite chair. "I am Francesco Cornaro, nephew of the Queen of Cyprus."

"I'm aware," said the elderly man.

"And you are?"

"I am Abraham, son of Moses Jaffe of Bologna."

"And you now reside...?"

"Wherever I am welcome."

Cornaro leaned back in his chair and contemplated what to ask this man. He could ask about his past to understand his experiences in life, thus what motivated the man. He could ask about a biblical text to understand the man's philosophies on religion. But considering he was a Jew with safe investments, Cornaro assumed he was motivated by money. Since his father's name was Moses Jaffe, he'd probably been a rabbi forced to relocate from Eastern Europe in the 1450s during a pogrom. Cornaro guessed the Jew's age to be near sixty, thus he may have been an infant when his family relocated to Bologna. In 1506, Bologna became a papal state, making a refugee of this man.

"Where have you been residing for the past four years?"

"Here, in the Soave valley. There is a small liberated community. We produce cheese. I provide for the castle kitchens."

"Liberated? Explain."

Abraham looked down and folded his hands in his lap. Then he placed his hands on his knees and stared straight at Cornaro. "We read from the Torah."

"You are aware that Maximilian, the Holy Roman Emperor, has decreed that all Jewish texts are to be destroyed?"

"I trust you will not inform Maximilian of my activities," Abraham said. "I trust you do not inform Maximilian of any activities?"

Cornaro sipped his wine. Who was interrogating who? Did Paolo say something that inferred doubt in Cornaro's loyalty to Venice? Did Paolo trust this Jew more than he trusted Cornaro?

Abraham lifted his eyebrows and asked, "And do you believe that Maximilian is truly the Holy Roman Emperor?"

"Excuse me?"

"He was never crowned by the Pope. He broke the long-standing tradition requiring a papal coronation in order to be ordained the Holy Roman Emperor. The Warrior Pope believes he may simply proclaim things, and they are thus settled in the eyes of God. I disagree. No man may be ordained to carry the will of God if God has not blessed it in a sacred house. Maximilian holds no more power in the eyes of God than any soldier or nobleman."

"Or you," Cornaro said.

"There again we disagree, but we always will, so further discussion is pointless." Abraham finished his wine.

The Jew drank from one of Cornaro's six Venetian wine glasses. Cornaro found his vision restrained to the glow of the Venetian glass and he took several small, rapid breaths through his nose before speaking. "I see you do not wear the yellow badge indicating your faith."

"No," Abraham said. He stood and adjusted his leather waist belt over his simple brown wool tunic.

"It is required in the city of Venice."

"Are we in the city?"

"You are in the Republic of Venice."

"Are you going to arrest me for fraternizing with Christians? I understand that in the city of Venice, the Jewish-Christian relations are quite progressive and tolerant. Do you not agree with the diplomacy designed by the elder generation? Is not your father a prominent member of the government counsel?"

Cornaro permitted a thin smile to spread across his face. This Jew knew far too much about Venetian politics. He was not a simple cheese maker. Cornaro sat down his wine glass and stood. He nodded to a soldier who then opened the door.

Cornaro said, "Before you go. My commander says you've seen Maximilian's troops. How recently? And have you any idea of the size of his army?"

Abraham's gaunt cheeks gave way to a small laugh. "Ah, now you see my use. Yes, a week ago, when I made deliveries to Verona. His army far exceeds yours. You should ask Mother Venice for reinforcements."

"And to whom will you deliver your cheese if the Venetians are once again defeated?"

"I sell to the castle kitchens. My cheese will feed whoever occupies these walls. It's nothing personal. Just business. Isn't that what you Christians like to say? That's what they said to my father when they made us all wear the yellow 'O' of insignificance. They said it symbolized that we were nothing in the eyes of the Lord. We were empty. Simply an outline of a yellow circle with a vacant center. But they said it was nothing personal. Just business. I ask you, Francesco Cornaro, what business do you invest in?"

Abraham's thin legs, covered by patched, rough wool stockings, nimbly took the old man from the room with a speed that belied his age. Cornaro heard both the guard's solid footsteps on the stairs and the light steps of the old Jew's cloth shoes. His smell lingered in the room. It was of cow barns, hay, and sour, curdled milk. Cornaro wrinkled his nose. He'd ask the servants to scrub the bench where the Jew had sat.

The Jew concerned Cornaro. How much did he know? He used unusual words, like *diplomacy*, and spoke of Francesco's father. Did he know that Cornaro was attempting to negotiate with Maximilian? And what about the Jew's talk that Maximilian wasn't the Holy Roman Emperor? Was that code for saying that Maximilian wasn't truly a servant to the Pope? Was it encouragement that an alliance between the Republic of Venice and Maximilian, thus Europe, could be made against the Pope?

The warrior pope had rapidly marched across Italy, forcing one state after another under the papal thumb of power, thus damaging long-established trade routes and tariffs. Maximilian had conquered half of Northern Italy, which meant that the Pope had no need to invade because the Pope's servant, the Holy Roman Emperor, was invading on his behalf. But what if the Jew was right? What if Maximilian himself only used the title to request funds from the Pope and was conducting his own war?

Could Venice and Maximilian become allies, and then the full force of Europe could remove the Pope from power? But is that what Venice wanted? Italy was the home of the Renaissance. Nowhere in Europe were they as advanced in art, literature, and architecture, or the art of war, as they were in Italy. If Europe was permitted to invade, would the soul of Italy be lost? Or could they coexist? Would Europe dominate Italy? Could Jews and Christians coexist without one dominating the other?

Cornaro shook his head and drank more wine. It was like asking humans to remove the word "Revenge" from their vocabulary. They could not. The baggage of life experience, grudges, and disappointments influenced all future relationships and formed prejudices and beliefs.

Cornaro picked up the delicate wine glass that Abraham had drunk from and hurled it against the stone wall of the fireplace. He flinched at the loss of one of his six precious Venetian glasses. Why was drinking from the same glass as a Jew so disgusting to him?

He picked up a candle with a tall flame and walked over to the spot littered with glass shards. He knelt down with the candle. The flame danced across the myriad surfaces of the broken glass. He flicked the shards with his fingers, pushing them into a tighter and tighter gathering. Soon, the dense population of glass islands filled a small circle on the floor. The fire flared in each shard, reflecting off segments of red, gold, and pure clear glass.

Cornaro asked himself why he hated Jews. His own family had few dealings with them. Talking to Abraham, just now, was his first significant conversation with a Jew, ever, in his entire lifetime. Yet, when he entered the room, he reacted viscerally. And now this, the shattered wine glass.

Was it the innuendos the old man made? *What business did he invest in?* Was the Jew accusing Cornaro of investing in Christianity instead of humanity? Man required religion. Even if only to display humaniti's skills at architecture and art. Cornaro believed that investing in Christianity invested in humanity. From Cornaro's perspective, the Jews only invested in themselves.

Cornaro crossed the room and exited to the outside landing. He descended to the kitchens and into an underground tunnel where he lit a flambeau. He walked quickly, anxiously, and inhaled the stench of his wax-dipped torch. The air in the tunnel was stale. He coughed.

Why did his heart race at the mere thought of Paolo befriending this elderly gentleman? Or was it because his feet fell too rapidly on the loose dirt of the descending tunnel, and his torch burned away all the available oxygen? He clutched his chest. He was young, fit. His heart raced because he feared for Venice. Venice and her noble families were prone to excesses. They were simple prey for the Jews with their easy lending and high interest returns. Upon his sister's marriage, almost her entire dowry was used to pay off her husband's debt, otherwise he would have lost his palazzo to a Jew. But the Jews could not live amongst the nobles. At least that much had been established. Perhaps it should be established where all the Jews should live? It would be easier to control them.

The tight gathering of broken glass shards danced in his mind. Venice was a gathering of small islands. One should be designated for the Jews and the bridges locked at night. Yes. That could be easily accomplished.

He wondered how much debt Paolo's family had incurred. Paolo felt perfectly comfortable drinking and chatting openly with a Jew as if one had married into the Gradenigo family. Why did Paolo, who probably did know Jews, many Jews, feel so comfortable with them, and Cornaro, who did not engage with Jews, feel so betrayed?

Paolo was younger, yes, but no more trusting. He was a skilled, ruthless military commander. Cornaro once witnessed Paolo fling a dagger from his belt into the neck of his Captain of Horse. A moment later Paolo rolled the body over and extracted a letter from the man's bloody doublet, revealing him to be a spy. If defending Mother Venice, Paolo ruthlessly suspected everyone of treason, even those loyal to him since birth. Cornaro assumed even he was routinely followed. Yet Paolo easily trusted this Jew. Why?

Cornaro stumbled on some loose stones in the tunnel pathway. He paused to regain his footing. What if he also decided to trust this Jew? Could one man change his prejudices against all Jews? He always felt like the instructor to his young friend, but perhaps this one time he might take a lesson from Paolo. In a time of war, perhaps in friendship, there might be something gained.

The tunnel ended and Cornaro stood in a small vaulted room with a fireplace to his left side. He lit three lanterns hanging from hooks in front of him and distributed them to hooks on the other three walls. He left his flaming flambeau in a cradle at the tunnel entrance, a black maw that represented his fear of the future, and unknown alliances.

He turned his attention to small barrels stacked on crates. He tapped on several, confirming they were full. He opened a small cask, one that could be carried on a man's shoulder, and sniffed the black powder inside. He nodded his approval at the slightly sulfurous, earthy smell. The gun powder was still dry.

The ten larger casks in the center of the room were not so nefarious, and the scent of yeast and alcohol wafted from their oak planks. They contained wine. Enough to supply a small Venetian army for a month. He admired whoever rolled the barrels down the tunnel, and he admired them even more for rolling them back up the tunnel at Paolo's request. He wondered if the kitchen staff knew about the gun powder or the crates of armor. Probably. But it wouldn't have surprised them considering the recent battle that had won Paolo the castle and the upcoming battle they would soon be forced into. Such items would be expected. It was the items on the other side of the fireplace he worried about; the chests of gold and jewels he might use to purchase mercenaries. Most importantly, he wondered how many people knew of the escape tunnel that led below the castle wall. The entrance to the escape tunnel was guarded by a monastery who adorned their halls with paintings by the Venetian masters Bellini and Mantegna, and sold their vegetables to the castle for ten times their worth.

He saw the Cornaro family crest burned into the top cork of a barrel and opened it. The sweet cherry and vanilla scents of his family's Cyprus vineyard reminded him why he was here. It reminded him of everything Venice had fought for and had died for over the past thousand years. Venice was the seat of sophistication, of art, of language, of learning, and no Jew was going to threaten that.

"Because he is older and wiser than me," Paolo answered when questioned by Cornaro about his new Jewish friend.

It was the next morning. Cornaro sipped his tea and nodded at a young boy who entered the breakfast room with a warm bread loaf.

"Nico," Paolo said to the boy as his small hands picked up a knife to slice the bread. "Did Abraham, the old man, deliver any cheese this morning? I'd love to enjoy it with the bread."

Nico nodded and ran back to the kitchen.

The bread filled the small room with the enticing aroma of toasted rosemary and olive oil. Nico arrived a few minutes later with a small plate of sliced cheese, dense with holes. "Have you tried it?" Paolo asked the boy. He shook his head. "Here. Taste it. Tell me if it's any good."

Nico tentatively took a slice of cheese from the plate and nibbled it. He smiled and took a bigger bite. "It's creamy," he said. "And salty and grassy. It's very good." Paolo offered him another slice, and the boy eagerly took it before returning to his post at the fireplace.

"Nico, can you please ask what's planned for dinner tonight?" Nico nodded and again ran from the room. Paolo leaned his head back to follow the boy's exit. He turned to Cornaro and said, "I use him as my taster, but I find that it's better if he doesn't know that. Two boys have already been poisoned."

"You don't trust the Jew's cheese?"

"Of course I do. It's difficult to poison cheese."

"So why haven't you eaten any of it yet?"

"I'm waiting for Nico to return with tonight's dinner menu. A good poisoner will use something with a delayed effect."

"But you trust the Jew?"

"Absolutely. However, two attempted poisonings in six months of occupying this fortress makes me a little restless. It would almost be easier if Maximilian simply attacked. The waiting is worse. Not to mention boring."

"The Jew said he saw Maximilian's army approaching Verona, only twenty miles from here."

"Is your father sending us reinforcements?" asked Paolo. "We cannot lose this fortress. If we lose Soave, we lose Venice."

"Maybe not."

"Cornaro, what have you been scheming? Do I need to dredge your fireplace ashes for burnt correspondence?"

"Hear me out. I too believe your new Jew friend has wisdom. He said things last night that made me believe we could form an alliance with Maximilian and the League of Cambria. Then we can use the forces of Europe to forever halt the warrior pope's progress into Northern Italy, thus securing the Republic of Venice."

"Never!" Paolo slammed his fist on the table.

Surprised by Paolo's anger, Cornaro asked, "Why?"

"An alliance will not secure the Republic of Venice, but only the League of Cambria. The League is half of Europe. We are a small, wealthy republic with an arsenal of ships and complete control over trade routes in the Eastern Mediterranean. We are the prize! Venice is the prize! An alliance would give the League everything our families built over the past thousand years."

Paolo tore off a bite of bread and chewed loudly, as he continued speaking, "And who are they? Barbarian tribes from France, Spain, and Germany?" Cornaro smirked as he brushed away flying bread crumbs from his sleeve. "Have you seen the recent paintings in the *Palazzo Ducale*? Nowhere in Europe does anything so beautiful exist. Would you be willing to end all the artistic progress hard won by Venice and her labors?"

Cornaro sipped his tea and pondered his young friend's sudden change in persuasive strategy. As of yesterday, Cornaro believed that Paolo considered a courtesan to be the highest form of art. He was quietly impressed with Paolo's new negotiating skills. This battle-strong, suspicious young man could one day become a diplomat. And this same young man, whom Cornaro admired, trusted a Jew. Perhaps Cornaro could suspend his prejudices.

Cornaro said, "I hear that Rome has also been successful in the world of art—"

His teacup clattered in its saucer as Paolo slammed his fist again on the table and shouted, "If you invite the League of Cambria—allow me to rephrase—offer up Venice like a plate of sardines, then Venice and all of Italy, including Rome, will be devoured."

"Europeans, no matter how barbaric, will never sack Venice or Rome," Cornaro said.

"Ha! Famous last words," said Paolo.

Nico returned, his cheeks flushed. Paolo turned his attention toward the boy, who rattled off the dinner menu for the evening and asked, "Cook wants to know if you can choose another barrel of wine to be brought up?" Paolo nodded, and Nico ran off again.

Paolo then reached for a slice of cheese and ate it atop the warm bread.

"Humm, it is grassy. And very creamy." Paolo said this as if they'd never been arguing. "You should definitely try it. It's not poisoned."

"I'm only concerned that Maximilian will defeat you in the coming battle. If he is open to an alliance, we would be fools not to attempt diplomacy."

"That is your father speaking. He convinced his own sister, the Queen of Cyprus, to donate her entire country to Venice. If diplomacy is the route required, then I trust your father. The man can persuade a goat to eat rock. But against the League of Cambria, no, there will be no diplomacy. They have no appreciation for art and culture." Paolo ate more cheese. "Or excellent cheese and wine. I bet that aged Cyprus wine would be wonderful with this." He chewed and drank tea. "Maximilian only knows conquest. He's only interested in increasing his power, wealth, and lands."

"And what are you interested in?" Cornaro asked. The intoxicating smells of the cheese and bread caused his stomach to grumble.

"Maintaining. I do not conquer, I defend. And this cheese is worth defending. Really, you should eat this. I hear your stomach grumbling."

Cornaro declined the Jewish cheese but took a slice of bread.

"Look at it this way," Paolo continued. "Abraham is earning an honest living. He's a dairy farmer and a cheese maker. He's not lending money. He's providing wages to his community and producing a quality product. I should ask him to ship some of this back to Venice. If you object to the usury practices of the Jews, then Abraham can cause you no objection. He's a good man. Eat."

"He has large investments in Cyprus. He lends. I just don't know who he lends to."

Paolo laughed. "So you don't like him because he's wealthy? Does that mean you hate all of your friends, including me?"

"You're not wealthy."

"Cornaro, either eat this cheese or leave. Your honesty always sours my stomach."

Cornaro refilled his teacup, took two more slices of bread, and left the room to the master of Soave Castle.

Once Cornaro was gone, Paolo called for Nico. "Can you please put some cheese and jam on a small plate and take it to Cornaro's room with a fresh pot of tea and some additional bread? Thank you." Paolo grinned to himself and ate more cheese.

❧

THAT AFTERNOON, Cornaro again traversed the half-mile underground tunnel connecting the castle to the secret wine vault. But unlike last night, he heard voices as he got closer to the entrance. He touched the stone wall of the tunnel, inhaled the dirt, and listened to happy mumblings and clinking glasses. It was Paolo and the old Jew. He heard Paolo say, "And he refused to taste your cheese. But fear not, I sent some to his room!"

Cornaro stepped into the vault.

"What is he doing here?" Cornaro demanded, his eyes wide and hand clenching the flambeaux.

"Cornaro!" Paolo said. "You're just in time. Abraham and I are picking out a wine barrel to best accent his cheese. Have you tried it yet? The cheese? If not, I have some here." Paolo bit into another thin slice.

Cornaro immediately realized his mistake of making the vault appear important. If the Jew was here, then Paolo must have downplayed its use. Paolo must have presented it as simply a wine cellar, not a vault for chests of gold, barrels of gunpowder, and a secret escape tunnel behind a false fireplace. He unclenched his grip, turned to rest his torch in a wall cradle, and took a breath. Lowering the tenor of his voice, Cornaro said, "Abraham, you mentioned you had investments in Cyprus wine. Perhaps you are familiar with some of the vineyards that Lord Gradenigo is so fond of."

"Indeed, I am," Abraham said, then sipped his wine. "This is one of my own. I believe it perfectly underscores the cheese. Are you sure you won't try some?"

Cornaro raised a hand to decline. Abraham shook his head in resignation.

"Exactly my thought," said Paolo, again with too much enthusiasm. Cornaro glared at him. "Did I not mention this wine to you this morning, Cornaro?" He leaned into the old Jew and said, "But this morning, I had no idea it was your vineyard. That explains why it is so perfectly matched to the cheese. You are a culinary genius, and a friend worth preserving. You must visit Venice."

Cornaro's hands clenched into fists again at hearing Paolo give such a compliment to this Jew.

Paolo tilted his head at Cornaro and asked, "What brings you here, Cornaro?"

"I wished to discuss a matter of business and was told to seek you here. I thought you were alone. I'll leave you." As Cornaro turned, he felt his eyes flit toward the fireplace, which was charred and looked realistic. Would it fool the Jew? The vault sat underneath a palazzo in the southeast corner of the walled city of Soave and had no access except for the tunnel from the castle and the tunnel from the monastery. Would the Jew assume it was vented through the fireplace? Would he ask? How would Paolo respond? The air was stagnate, but not foul. The Jew was smart. Would he wonder how the torches and lanterns remained lit? But Paolo was also smart.

Cornaro exited, but remained in the darkness of the castle tunnel. He leaned on the tunnel wall and fingered the jagged cut stones. Paolo and Abraham happily babbled on about wines and cheeses. Their laughs echoed off the vaulted ceiling and walls. Paolo's behavior was perfectly acceptable and no military secrets were being divulged. Abraham's conversation was convivial. Perhaps they knew Cornaro was listening?

He walked back to the castle and to his room. He waited on a scout to return with news of Maximilian's army. His own father had entered into negotiations with Maximilian and the League of Cambria, but Cornaro hadn't received any correspondence from Venice in three days. However, that morning he wrote to his father about Paolo's objections to an alliance and concern that regardless of his father's efforts, Paolo would never surrender the castle.

∾

CORNARO'S BEDROOM window opened to the night air. Flames flickered outside. Smoke filled Cornaro's nose and throat. He coughed. He dropped to the floor of his room and crawled into the hallway and then to the neighboring bedroom.

The hall guards were gone. The castle courtyard echoed with sword clatter and shouting. The smoke thickened above him.

How did Maximilian's army breach the castle's defenses? On his hands and knees, Cornaro reached for the door handle to Paolo's bedroom. He pushed it open, but couldn't find Paolo. He shouted for him. An arrow sunk into the wooden door above his head.

"Cornaro! Come with me."

Cornaro turned and saw Paolo standing behind him. Paolo rushed to him and wrapped a wet cloth around Cornaro's face. "Breathe through this. I must get you out or your father will never forgive me."

"How did they get in?" Cornaro asked. He stood and leaned over the railing to assess the damage and swordplay below.

"A small army penetrated, killed the gate guards, and opened the front gate. Maximilian's army simply walked in."

"But how?"

"I don't know. It doesn't matter now. The castle is lost. We must retreat and protect Venice. To the tunnel. Now! Come with me."

Cornaro coughed and put his hand over the wet cloth covering his mouth. The smell of burnt hair filled his nose. Paolo hit Cornaro's shoulder and head.

"Sorry about that. You were smoldering. You might consider a wig when you get back to Venice. Or a very short haircut." Paolo's voice sounded muffled, like he was shouting through a wall. Cornaro realized that Paolo also wore a thick wet cloth across his face.

Cornaro wanted to laugh but could only cough. Paolo had his arm around Cornaro's waist and guided him down a staircase. At the landing, a man with a spear rushed by, followed by another man, yelling with primal rage, his arm bleeding, and swinging a sword overhead.

"Good man!" Paolo gave a muffled yell. "Never surrender!"

The smoke decreased as they descended, and Cornaro was able to recover his breathing after another downward flight. Once they reached the kitchens, he felt fully recovered.

Paolo looked at him, "Are you okay? Oh damn!"

"What?"

"I forgot to grab those jeweled slippers you love. Should I go back?"

Cornaro laughed. "I need you conscious right now. Otherwise, I'd hit you. Hard." They both laughed. Cornaro marked the moment in his memory. It had been a long time since they had laughed together. He said, "Lead the way."

They ran down the cool, damp tunnel. The sounds of battle, fury, and screams of death faded away behind them. Not wanting to imagine the horrors that they alone were escaping, Cornaro attempted to keep the mood light. "We should have packed some of Abraham's cheese. We have a long night ahead of us, and it's very good."

"Cornaro! I'm so proud of you. You finally respect him as a person. I quite enjoy his company."

As they got closer to the secret vault, the air of the tunnel smelled fresher than usual and Paolo's torch fire flared with fresh oxygen. A moment too late, Cornaro's mind calculated their mistake.

They entered the vault, but were not alone. There, in the darkness, stood Abraham. The dim light from the single torch silhouetted six armed soldiers.

"Abraham?" Paolo's voice trembled with anger and betrayal.

Abraham stepped backward and the six soldiers drew their swords. Paolo leaped into the room, his sword drawn, and in a swift blow, decapitated the nearest soldier.

Cornaro gasped when the head rolled near his feet.

The other five soldiers jumped into action. Paolo injured two more and Cornaro reached toward the headless man to procure his sword.

Another soldier stabbed a sword into Paolo's side, then gurgled blood as Cornaro's sword thrust through his neck. As the soldier fell, he pulled out the sword from Paolo's side, releasing a trickle of blood. It flowed down his side and leg. Cornaro grabbed him, attempting to staunch the flow with his hands, but the blood only seemed to increase. Paolo collapsed into him. Cornaro fell to the ground, holding his commander. Paolo raised his sword in defense against another attack, but a standing solder knocked Paolo's sword from his weakened grip.

Abraham put his hands on the last two soldiers and shook his head. "Please, let me," he said. The two soldiers stepped back.

Paolo looked up at his friend, Abraham, and asked, "Why? You're aiding those who despise you?"

"I must protect my investment. Your friend Cornaro understands. I'm a lender, and I've lent large sums to the League of Cambria. If I can help ensure that I will be repaid, then I must do so. It's not personal. It's just business."

"You waited here so you could kill me?"

"I must thank you for showing me this room."

Paolo turned his head to look up at Cornaro. "It's all my fault."

"Signore Gradenigo," said the Abraham. His knees cracked as he knelt down to take Paolo's hand. "Do not blame yourself. It was your friend who doomed you. Beware the company you keep."

Cornaro saw Paolo's hand go limp and fall to the floor. Cornaro's leg was warm from Paolo's blood, which now pooled and flowed around the limp hand. Still trying to staunch the flow, Cornaro adjusted his hand. He held his friend's dead body and cried out. The loss he felt sank into his chest like a hot iron.

"If you had been kind, like your young friend, I would have let both of you live." The torch flame flickered in the dark eyes of the Jew as he and Cornaro glared at each other. The Jew continued, "There were no drafts and the fireplace has no chimney, so the burnt back wall was an obvious hidden door. I feigned concerned for one of the barrels and crawled around the base of it to examine the ties. That's when I noticed that the fireplace chimney ended at the stone vaulted ceiling. From there, it was only a matter of finding the tunnel entrance beyond the castle wall, which would be in a protected place of some distance. I trade cheese and ale with both the local monasteries. I remembered a strange door in a kitchen larder of one of those monasteries. A few months ago, I set my cheese down on a shelf and thought, 'What a strange place for a door. I wonder where it goes?' Yesterday, I opened that door, and guess what I found? A tunnel to here. I'd like to thank you for the gold. It will certainly help repay the many debts Maximilian has accrued, particularly his debts to me."

Cornaro reached for Paolo's sword, but the Jew kicked it away.

"Signore Cornaro, I must also thank you and your family for your generous correspondence. My father never wrote me letters with such high praise for my efforts, but your father is certainly proud of you. And I particularly enjoyed the letter you wrote him yesterday, stating that you were worried your young friend would never surrender the castle, despite your father's efforts to form an alliance with the Holy Roman Emperor, Maximillian."

Cornaro remained on the floor, silent.

"Are you confused? I'll explain. If an alliance is formed between Venice and Maximilian, then my loans are immediately repaid and I would be deprived of an enormous profit in interest. Taking the castle perpetuates the war and engenders the highest profit to me. If the battle continues, I continue to accrue interest on my loans. As even you can observe, it's just business."

"And what of my father's efforts? You do not speak for Maximilian," Cornaro said.

"What efforts? I intercepted your father's letters to Maximilian. He knows nothing of Venice's offer for peace. But if you'd like to propose it, please let me know." He waved a soldier over. The soldier laid the point of his blade at Cornaro's neck.

Cornaro sat very still, sweating in the cold room. Then he snapped. No more thinking. Thinking, doubting, questioning, had gotten Paolo killed. He grabbed the sword blade at his neck and tried to shove it in. The soldier yanked the blade away, slicing the palm of Cornaro's hand.

"No, no," said the Jew with a sad sigh. "Cornaro, I'd like you to go back to Venice and tell your father and uncle and the Council of Ten what happened here. Tell them how your friend died in your arms. Tell them that your harsh reaction to me in the vault gave away the secret that this room was more than it appeared to be. Paolo was a good host, a proper, kind, and appreciative host to me. If you hadn't entered here and created tension, I would never have suspected anything. But you set off my senses. Maybe next time, you'll follow Paolo's example and be kinder to Jews."

"You killed him!"

"No, Cornaro. You did. Your unjustified hatred of my kind caused me to sniff out the tunnels and lead Maximilian's army directly into your castle keep. Venice has lost Soave because of you. Paolo has died because of you. I want you to think about that."

The Jew walked over to the fireplace wall and opened it. A gust of fresh air hit Cornaro's face and stung his bleeding hand.

"Stand," the Jew commanded. A soldier pulled Paolo off Cornaro, and another soldier lifted Cornaro to his feet.

Cornaro gaped at the carnage in the small room; tangled limbs, contorted faces, and two disembodied heads. Paolo's blood pooled into a thick puddle at his feet. Cornaro bent down, pressed his bleeding hand into the puddle, and whispered, "Never surrender." The soldier behind him poked his back with a sword. Cornaro stood up, grimaced at the smell of hay and sour milk emanating from the Jew's rough tunic, and said, "If I have killed my friend, then you have killed your kind." He walked through the fireplace, and entered the tunnel to the monastery with new determination to destroy the League of Cambria and imprison all Jews.

INSPIRATION FOR THE SECRET VAULT

*O*n my first visit to Venice in 2005, I was shocked by the fact that the leading cosmopolitan trading city of the Renaissance, with its extreme religious tolerance—by 16th century standards—established the first Jewish ghetto. Actually, the first was in Frankfurt, Germany, but the second was in Venice, and the Venetian ghetto became the template for all other ghetto's around the world. The word "ghetto" was founded by Venice, as *ghèto* was the word for the copper foundry that originally stood on the small seven acre island in the Cannaregio district, which in 1516, became the *Gheto Novo*, or New Ghetto.

In the 15th and 16th century, Venice was a safe haven for Jewish refugees escaping many parts of Europe, including other regions of Italy. Jews were allowed to operate businesses in Venice, but were not allowed to reside in Venice. In this story, I speculated that the patricians, the noble families of Venice, often led by Francesco Cornaro's father, Giorgio Cornaro (1452-1527, aka: Corner), might have had personal financial reasons for suppressing Jewish freedom. The wealth of the Cornaro/Corner family was created by their money-lending practices, amongst other pursuits. I speculated that if Giorgio Cornaro's son returned with a story of military loss and murder, orchestrated by a Jew, then it might persuade the other members in the Council of Ten to continue their suppression of Jews and oppose residency.

However, in 1516, the Jewish community in Venice negotiated for residency within the city of Venice, and the Senate designated the old copper foundry, the *ghèto*, as a Jewish residence and the bridge gates surrounding the island were locked each night. It was an interesting way to simultaneously include and exclude the Jews from Venetian society. After only twelve short years, the Jews felt secure enough in their new residence to build synagogues, so even if they had to wear a yellow insignia or hat to distinguish themselves from Christians, Jews embraced their city residence. Their community grew, and they created more living spaces by building upwards on their small prison island.

I speculated that the old Venetian Patrician families were not anti-Semitic, but felt financially threatened by some of the Jewish merchants and moneylenders. Many of the Patrician families owned and operated banks. Several other powerful families had amassed enormous debts, and some were indebted to Jews. Suppressing the Jews meant maintaining power within the wealthy Patrician class.

The fabulous Castle of Soave really did have a tunnel connecting its main keep to a wine vault. Whether an additional tunnel led from the vault, under the city wall, and eventually opened in a monastery a half mile away, is speculative based on other European castles where such escape tunnels existed.

The general outline of the events in this story is true. Maximillian I, who the Warrior Pope, Julius II (Papal reign 1503-13–the Pope who tortured Michelangelo under a famous ceiling), declared as the Holy Roman Emperor without a proper church coronation, led the League of Cambria, essentially armies gathered from Europe, against Northern Italy. Soave Castle was a stronghold protecting the Veneto region and Venice from invasion. The castle is a gorgeous sight to behold, especially at sunrise or sunset. You should check it out and partake in some excellent wine tasting within the walled city of Soave.

From the history page of the castle's website:

https://www.castellodisoave.it/en

> *It was the year 1509 when the army of the Lega di Cambrai, led by imperor Massimiliano I° d'Asburgo, defeated the fortress resistance.*
>
> *Short after, the castle was regained by Venetians guided by Paolo Gradenigo, but just until the spring of 1510, when the imperial troops reconquered it.*
>
> *In September of the same year, Soave's people, led by Antonio Marogna, revolted and after, as chronicle states, 'having chopped to pieces' the imperial guards they handed over the fortress to the Venetians by opening its doors.*

Massimiliano I, d'Asburgo (aka: Maximillian I of the house of Habsburg) passed the "Imperial Confiscation Mandate," which ordered the destruction of all Jewish literature apart from the Bible. So, did a Jew really work for him? Yes!

The character of Abraham is a real figure from history. Abraham ben Moses Jaffe of Bohemia (1450-1535) was a prominent 16th century Bohemian Jewish banker and money lender and lent money to European and German royalty and nobility—like the House of Habsburg—in exchange for social privileges. He is known to have leant money to Maximilian I during the League of Cambria wars. It is also true that Abraham's mother, Margolioth bat Samuel HaLevi, was considered an extremely educated woman, and so respected in the Jewish community that some of her descendants, like Abraham's brother, adopted the second surname Margolioth.

Instead of following his mother's example of studied wisdom, in 1512 he persuaded the King of Poland to pronounce him Prefect over the Jewish community and to become the tax collector for the Jewish poll tax in Poland. This enriched both the King and Abraham. The Jewish community of Kraków was so disgusted by Abraham's mistreatment of his own people, they banned him from their society. In retaliation, the King ordered all the Jews of Poland, and especially the rabbis, to respect the liberties and privileges granted to Abraham, and not to encroach upon these liberties by excommunication or in any other such way. I imagine this did not endear Abraham to the Jewish communities. For the story, I speculated that Abraham was a man who solely protected his own self-interest and not that of the Jewish community, as his historical actions demonstrated shortly after the battle at Soave in 1510.

Pope Julius II despised all things Jewish, except perhaps Jewish doctors, as it's rumored the Pope had a Jewish doctor whom Michelangelo befriended. Fun fact, Pope Julius II's uncle, Pope Sixtus, was so anti-Semitic, he commissioned the Sistine Chapel in the same dimensions as the Temple of Solomon so it could be *re-birthed* as a new Catholic Chapel. Maximilian I and Pope Julius II's mutual hatred of Jews is possibly why they bonded so well and the Pope saw it fit to proclaim him the "Holy Roman Emperor" from a distance. The irony is that it was Maximilian's son, Charles V, and his mutinous army, who sacked Rome in 1527.

When in Venice, be sure to admire one of the Cornaro homes, Palazzo Corner della Ca' Grande, which was designed by Alexis Lynn's favorite Renaissance architect, Jacopo Sansovino. There are several Cornaro (Corner) palazzos, but Ca' Grande located between the Accademia Bridge and St. Mark's square is the most magnificent. It was commissioned by Francesco Cornaro's cousin—His father was dead, it wasn't his brother, so I'm guessing a cousin. The Cornaro family uses the same first names over and over again, so the family tree gets a little confusing—after the original Cornaro family home at the same Grand Canal location was destroyed by a fire in 1532.

While visiting Venice or Northern Italy, I highly recommend a day trip to Soave. The landscape is breathtaking and the wine is delicious. And perhaps you'll meet a ghost from one of the many bloody battles fought within Castello di Soave.

AFTERWORD

Lord Byron not only absorbed the history around him, he swam in it. Sometimes literally. Whether it was in England, Venice, or Greece, he used history for inspiration in his poetry and stories.

From the Preface of his play, *Marino Faliero, Doge of Venice, An Historical Tragedy in Five Acts*, Lord Byron writes:

 Marino Faliero amongst the Doges, and the Giants' Staircase, where he was crowned, and discrowned, and decapitated, struck forcibly upon my imagination; as did his fiery character and strange story. I went, in 1819, in search of his tomb more than once to the church San Giovanni e San Paolo; and, as I was standing before the monument of another family, a priest came up to me and said, "I can show you finer monuments than that." I told him that I was in search of that of the Faliero family, and particularly of the Doge Marino's. "Oh," said he, "I will show it you;" and, conducting me to the outside, pointed out a sarcophagus in the wall with an illegible inscription. He said that it had been in a convent adjoining, but was removed after the French came, and placed in its present situation; that he had seen the tomb opened at its

removal; there were still some bones remaining, but no posi-
tive vestige of the decapitation.

My own visits to Venice also became research expeditions, as something would strike my imagination and I would pursue it methodically and exhaustively, sometimes to the annoyance of my husband. Being an artist, he was usually a good sport for artistic deep dives, but on a rare occasions he would park himself at a café alongside a pleasant canal and declare, "No more churches today. I'm done."

Also from the same Preface, Lord Byron writes:

> *In speaking of the drama of Marino Faliero, I forgot to mention that the desire of preserving ... has induced me to represent the conspiracy as already formed, and the Doge acceding to it; whereas, in fact, it was of his own preparation and that of Israel Bertuccio. The other characters (except that of the Duchess), incidents, and almost the time, which was wonderfully short for such a design in real life, are strictly historical, except that all the consultations took place in the palace. Had I followed this, the unity would have been better preserved; but I wished to produce the Doge in the full assembly of the conspirators, instead of monotonously placing him always in dialogue with the same individuals. For the real facts, I refer to the Appendix.*

Lord Byron thought it important to represent the accurate history of an event if the details had been known or documented, and with the case of Doge Marino Faliero, his tragic affairs were documented. As stated above, Lord Byron admits to taking some dramatic license, but otherwise, it's a pretty accurate history.

He wrote to his publisher, John Murray in February 1817, "I want it, and can not find so good an account of that business here.... I have searched all [Venice's] histories; but the policy of the old aristocracy made their writers silent on [Faliero's] motives, which were a private grievance against one of the patricians."

One of the thrills of historical research is finding a story with documented bits and pieces, but missing many of the details. This allows me to hypothesize relationships and motivations to fill in the blanks, but still remain true to the larger historical events. It's a fun way to bring history back to life and to remember the smaller figures whom the archives have hidden, or who might only appear in a painting, or be remarked on in a letter. Women in particular, like Marietta Robusti, have been largely forgotten, but she was vital to the success of Tintoretto's studio.

I hope you've enjoyed my stories filled with *could have, would have,* or *might have* happened scenarios. If they inspire you to explore a museum, archive, or your grandparent's library, then I hope you find a story that tickles your interest and invites all your senses to dive into a historical tale that grabs hold of you and won't let go. Who knows, a little research, a few lost letters, an old drawing, and you might just bring someone back to life. And that's magical.

ACKNOWLEDGMENTS

I'm excited to announce that two of these stories will appear in Kaye Booth's Fall 2022 WordCrafter anthology, *Visions*. Kaye has edited anthologies with legends Kevin J. Anderson and Jonathan Maberry. Thank you Kaye, for all your Beta reads and inviting me into your author world.

I lift a Venetian wine glass to Elisabeth for her editing assistance. Your notes and ideas are always brilliant. Keep them coming. How you find the time to do everything you do, I will never know. I gift a bottle of Soave to my favorite writing partner, Kris, who has promised to retire to Europe with me. Can we retire now?

To Auntie Kathleen, my favorite art historian, thanks for your confidence boost and art advice after reading the early drafts of the art history stories. Warning, when I write my Renaissance artist spy series, I'm going to bombard your brain for fun art history tidbits.

Thank you Mom for always asking me about my latest historical pursuits. You make me feel like I'm not crazy for caring about all these dead people.

To my husband for his encouragement to write a short story every week. Your deadlines prevented me from falling down the rabbit hole of historical research. I can't thank you enough for discussing medieval plagues and Venetian sewer system with me like they were common dinner conversations. And thanks for being such a fabulous chef. I will always wash the dishes.

ABOUT THE AUTHOR

Sara W. McBride is a grown-up child and many of her adult party conversations end with a comical defense of why her first degree in theater from UCLA, and her second degree in molecular biology from SDSU, are completely related. Between her degrees, she spent two years pranking the mafia in New York City architecture; also completely related.

All parts of her life have led her down a streamlined path toward noveling because nothing else maintains her sanity. Like many modern-day biological researchers, she spent years inventing new swear words to sling at million-dollar machines while locked in dark holes of decaying academic halls. This caused her to witness ghosts and create a romantic fantasy life within her head, which she now scribbles down on very non-technological paper with her favorite Jane Austen style quill pen.

Sara now enjoys a new career in beer brewing. It's awesome!

When not getting paid to drink beer, she's hard at work on the second Alexis Lynn novel with a second collection of historical stories inspired by the legends and castles of Venice and the Veneto. Also in the works is a Regency mystery series and a haunted play. She strongly feels the world needs more haunted plays.

When not researching hops and malts, reading history, or writing in random, elegant hotel lobbies, she's hiking the San Diego shore-lines with her husband and their tiny, bouncy dog named Wombat. However, she dreams of living in Venice and is open to any offers to organize ancestral archives.

ALSO BY SARA WESLEY MCBRIDE

Will Write for Wine: Alexis Lynn and the Romance of Venice

If you've read these stories, but not the novel, then go read the novel to watch characters fight over the stories you just read.

www.ingramcontent.com/pod-product-compliance
Lightning Source LLC
Chambersburg PA
CBHW052135170626
46812CB00004B/1436